THE BEST OF ALL WORLDS

Voltaire was a brilliant satirist, but not even Voltaire could satirize what he never knew. This book does it for him. Beginning a couple of hundred years after *Candide* left off, *The Best of All Worlds* describes exactly that: in other words, the world today — and attacks with relish certain aspects of it which at one time or another are criticized by most thinking people.

7

HANS JØRGEN LEMBOURN

THE BEST OF
ALL WORLDS

or, WHAT VOLTAIRE NEVER KNEW

Translated from the Danish
by EVELYN RAMSDEN

with drawings by
GUNVOR ÖVDEN EDWARDS

G. P. PUTNAM'S SONS
NEW YORK

Library of Congress Catalogue Number 61-9179
Manufactured in the United States of America

CONTENTS

In the course of writing this book I have received much valuable assistance. I should like to thank the author for permission to quote part of the song about what the sailor said to the nun. A psychiatrist has given me a great deal of constructive comment which has been of great use to me. The same applies to a cook, a Member of Parliament, and a publisher. But above all I should like to thank M. François-Marie Arouet de Voltaire for the courageous scepticism with which he viewed the best of all possible worlds, despite the fact that this scepticism cost him exile and most of his friends.

H.J.L.

CHAPTER ONE

Count Frederick is instructed in two opposing views of life, after which he allows himself to be seduced with a result which surprises him greatly.

COUNT FREDERICK CHRISTIAN PEDER WESSEL ULRIK-ULRIKKENFELDT of Egeborg had a shock of fair hair, blue eyes, and a face which, despite being almost always amiable, was never irritating.

Thanks to heredity and a good, sensible middle-class education, he had become a very pleasant sort of young man. But while he had been taught that good manners were likely to please and inspire confidence, he had not been warned that to the more revolutionary-minded such manners act like a challenge, and this later proved his undoing. But it was his parents' fault: they knew no better.

That he was furthermore endowed with an inborn simplicity (coupled with an unrestrained curiosity which he had apparently inherited from the founder of his line in the thirteenth century) was another serious disadvantage: for this simplicity was destined to complicate his existence to a remarkable degree, since it caused him to suffer from a child-like desire to be honest, which now and then hindered him from enjoying to the full the pleasures of the best of all possible worlds.

Count Frederick was a good-looking young man, but that did not mean he was effeminate, or a mollycoddle, or a mother's darling. Of course, it is not altogether an advantage to be a good-looking young man when there are so few of them; but Count Frederick possessed just that combination of qualities that in a more romantic and less envious world might have provided him with a very pleasant existence of the kind portrayed in gay, sophisticated film comedies.

Now the young man's tutor, Mr Engelsen, M.A., had

contributed very largely to the formation of his character. This Mr Engelsen was a Marxist.

'But,' asked Count Frederick one day, 'is it due to some personal deficiency that I am a count and the heir to a castle and over two thousand acres of good arable land, as well as five hundred head of cattle of the very best breeds?'

'That will adjust itself,' answered Engelsen, 'although I admit the adjustment may not help your understanding of public welfare — which is undoubtedly the main thing. But if it is any consolation to you, I can assure you that the State will gradually relieve you of your burden, divide up the two thousand five hundred acres, turn your private bathing-beach into a public breathing-space, and make the castle into a splendid museum, of which you may be appointed custodian at a fixed salary and a pension. So don't let it get you down.'

'Would it not be better if a benevolent State were to act at once, so that I am not exposed to temptation any longer than is absolutely necessary?'

'Not at all, my boy. It is your duty to bring the yield of the estate and farm up to such a pitch that everyone can see how preposterous it is for a single man to earn so much. At that point it will be obvious that the State is doing the community a necessary service by taking over, and all will feel that a great injustice has been righted. So everything will turn out for the best all round.'

'But isn't it very amusing to earn a lot of money?' asked Count Frederick.

'One must not think only of oneself, my boy.'

'No, of course not, Mr Engelsen, but I can well imagine that it would be very amusing, all the same. I think it would be much more amusing than thinking of others. Have you never thought so?'

'What an idea!'

'It is only that I felt that surely you ought not to be living here in the castle at a very high salary and with so little work to do. With your ideas, I mean. And when the State at last takes notice of my progressive degeneracy, you won't be anything like as comfortably off. It struck me that perhaps you thought that it was amusing to get as much as you could for as long as you could.'

Mr Engelsen, who had grown very plump lately, laughed richly and heartily. The well-proportioned echo compartment of his stomach made his laughter particularly convincing.

'My boy, your training in logic is still woefully incomplete. Surely you understand that I am employed in work of extreme national importance in initiating you, and only you, into the blessings of communal ownership, so that you may not become embittered from sheer lack of understanding of the proper significance of things. I do not deny that I receive a fairly high salary, but as it is so important to help in the maximum possible division of material wealth, I am acting in the true spirit of Marxism when I draw my salary on the first of each month. Besides, I am making great sacrifices by exposing myself to the temptations of easy living here in the castle. And all to advance the public good. We socialists are the first to co-ordinate theory and reality. We have discovered the best of all possible theories, and we are now well on the way to achieving the best of all possible societies, thus showing that theory and reality are one and the same. If there are occasional minor discords, they are no more than temporary little difficulties on the way towards the perfect society in which we shall all be equal and therefore all happy.

'All misery and evil in this world are due to the fact that, contrary to nature's intentions, some people are different from others. We both have a nose and a sense of smell, for instance, and this sense of smell reacts equally to good and bad odours. So it must be meant that we should both smell the same smells; otherwise we should have been given different senses of smell, shouldn't we? We both have a tongue and a palate with nerves of taste, and both your and my taste nerves prefer eighteen small well-cleaned oysters with one and a half dessertspoonfuls of Worcester sauce mixed with five drops of Tabasco sauce, two tablespoonfuls of tomato ketchup, two teaspoonfuls of lemon juice and half a saltspoonful of cayenne pepper, to a good plateful of porridge. Don't you agree? Ergo, it must be intended that we should all eat oyster-cocktails and not only some of us. So everything is fundamentally good as it is, and only a few small improvements and adjustments are needed here and there.'

Count Frederick's parents had died in a car crash when he was twelve years old, and his grandfather, Count Hector, had then taken charge of him. Count Hector's most out-standing feature was his nose. He had one of those large, overhanging beaks that betoken a powerful and unusual mind of the kind that might have made him a highly-prized general in Napoleon's army if he had only lived a century earlier. This, of course, he had not done; instead, he was very much present in the twentieth, and he instructed Count Frederick principally in the profits likely to accrue from prize cows and pedigree bulls.

'Unhappily we can none of us avoid the misfortune of being alive,' he said, 'but if your income is large enough you can at least have the satisfaction of choosing those forms of misfortune that suit you best.' And, having said that much, he handed over the rest of Count Frederick's upbringing to Engelsen.

'I cannot understand,' Count Frederick said to his grand-father, 'how you, with your attitude to life, can allow me to be influenced by Engelsen.'

'Everything exists by contraries and only by contraries,' answered Count Hector, 'and I am assuming that you have inherited sufficient natural cussedness to adopt a point of view that is the exact opposite of that held by those responsible for your upbringing.'

'Aren't you running a great risk?'

Count Hector scratched his nose violently and looked

searchingly at his grandson. 'No,' he said, 'I don't think I am.'

'But just suppose you wanted to teach me about something other than estimating my income, what sort of advice would you give me?'

'Hm! I suppose it can't do any harm, provided I make it short,' said Count Hector thoughtfully. 'Well now, first of all, always be natural. That means first and foremost that you should see to it that you are always in a position where it is possible to speak the truth. Only the man who stands alone can be absolutely truthful. Admittedly it takes a good deal of courage to stand alone — but try to do so. Besides, have you ever heard a dog or a cat or a cow tell a lie?

'Secondly, you should note that nature never allows the smallest patch of earth to be wasted. She arranges to bring forth a few weeds at least where nothing else can exist. What can you learn from that? Why, that if you follow nature's example in yourself, you will not waste anything either. Ideas are all very well, but nature is the most vigorous any day.

'Thirdly, you should never accept a gift unless you have either given, or are able to give in return, something that is of greater, or at least of equal, value. It is well known that corn never grows where it has not been sown.

'In other words — speak the truth, develop your natural gifts, never enjoy what you have not cultivated, and you will be a free man and possibly less discontented than most. And let me tell you in passing that the best of all gifts is the one that women can give. It is also the least lasting.'

Count Frederick had an opportunity to discover this for himself at the beginning of his sixteenth year when a luscious little peach called Pernille was installed in the castle. She had an atom-sized soul whose power-points were incapsulated in four melon-like globosities of about the same size and shape. She polished the floors and dusted the picture-frames, and both forms of occupation aroused great curiosity in Count Frederick's susceptible mind. When the two upper melons were pointing towards the ancestors on the walls of the banqueting hall, he felt a sort of dewily fresh sunrise in his loins, and when the two lower ones were reflected in the parquet floors, he noticed his mouth opening and shutting with a convulsive movement, the rhythm of which he was quite unable to control. His interest in the cleaning and polishing of the castle increased considerably, but he did not think that his naive inquiries in any way betrayed what was going on inside him, although some amazing things were. He found he could hear better, and see better, and taste things better, and long after he had spoken to Pernille a smiling grimace would remain on his features, which he only remembered when his jaw-muscles began to ache.

'Men in love are always laughable,' said Engelsen, when he realized what was happening to his pupil, 'for they try to be more charming than they really are.'

Then Engelsen, who was very fond of melons himself, added, 'You may learn from your present feelings that there is nothing greater than love of one's neighbour; and further, that consideration of rank or class, or any other barrier that might hinder this love, is of the devil.'

To Count Frederick this democratic theory was still purely theoretical. He had never had the opportunity to put it into practice, so he simply continued to be more charming than he really was and to endure his aching jaws afterwards. Consequently nothing really happened — until, one evening, Pernille entered his room. The Count had not been sleeping well of late, but in his confusion, now, he thought he must be dreaming.

'I just came in because I had forgotten to sweep under your bed,' said Pernille, sitting down on it, 'but there's no need to say any more, is there?'

She swayed backwards, and Count Frederick came near to losing consciousness. He suddenly found that he could no longer depend on his senses, which were making the two upper melons change their shape and turn into two trumpets blowing a wild reveille around him.

'W-w-w-one should always speak the t-t-t-truth,' he stuttered.

'Well — ?'

Count Frederick drew a deep breath and blinked his eyes rapidly until the melons became melons again. 'Among other things I've been wondering about for a long time,' he said, 'is whether those two stand out like that by themselves.'

'The best way to find out would be to feel them, wouldn't it?'

The Count blushed at the audacity of this conversation; but then he remembered that Engelsen had told him that everything that hindered him from loving his neighbour was of the devil, and he felt better. So he said: 'You are my neighbour, aren't you, Pernille?'

'You bet I am,' she answered.

So with hands that were born to estimate the value of all that was imaginatively planned and nobly created, Count Frederick confirmed that although this world (in spite of Engelsen's promises) was full of deception he could not at that moment desire more tangible proof to the contrary.

Nevertheless the Count had scruples, and, remembering Engelsen's teaching, he said: 'We can only be really happy when we are equal, and since you are Pernille and I am Count Frederick, it might be thought that your charming generosity springs from this unfortunate inequality, and that therefore unhappiness will result. Besides, I have been taught by my grandfather that one should never accept a gift unless one can return it with a still more magnificent one, or at least one equally good — and I can't see how I can possibly give you a more perfect gift than the one you are now about to give me.'

Pernille produced a few sounds from her strawberry mouth such as generally only kissing-fish make, shook her shining head vigorously and answered: 'Engelsen is no doubt a very wise man, especially if one interprets his words of wisdom according to the needs of the moment. But anyone looking at us could tell at once that I am not a countess, nor you a chauffeur. From what I've understood of Engelsen's teaching, everything in this world depends first and foremost on the outward and visible signs, and so far as they go, we shall both soon be looking very much alike. So you can keep your hair on. As for your grandfather's good advice, you will see in a few seconds that the gift you can give me will be worth quite as much as the gift I can give you.'

'Then everything seems to be just as we have both been taught,' sighed Count Frederick contentedly. 'Engelsen and my noble grandfather are both very wise men.'

'So far I've had no personal experience of your grandfather's wisdom,' answered Pernille, 'but Engelsen has taught me many things that are now going to benefit you.'

A little stab of jealousy forced its way into the Count's swelling heart when he heard this, but he soon forgot it and reminded himself that Pernille was Engelsen's neighbour too and that therefore all must be well.

After this Pernille showed him many different ways in which equality could be demonstrated, and when he woke the next morning, very late, he was full of contentment and tenderness.

Confused by the copious exchange of gifts during the next few weeks, Count Frederick suffered from a misapprehension not altogether unknown in such cases, and thought that the joy with which Pernille's melons filled him and his nights was what is commonly called love. She became in his eyes a baroness, a countess, and finally a fairy-tale princess with golden hair and a crown and the most exquisite manners, and he felt in his inmost being, now always so tired in the morning, that he loved her very much indeed. Then he began to worry whether the acrobatics with which he and Pernille demonstrated their deep feelings for each other might not have serious results. He already saw in imagination the tears on her rosy-apple cheeks, heard her noisy sobs and was soon regarding himself as a bungler and a cad. But then he comforted himself with delightful thoughts of all he would do for his beloved when she increased the family. Perhaps a royal dispensation could be obtained whereby the still hypothetical little count could be born of a countess. Indeed, he went so far in his imaginings that by the time he confessed his fears to Pernille in the morning, they were no longer fears, and he spoke in a voice full of devotion and pride over the imagined result.

But Pernille only laughed, scratched her navel, and said: 'Don't you worry about that.'

'Yes, but if ... '

'If, and if! You just kiss me. There. And there.'

Count Frederick kissed her, there, and there, and as usual became a little dizzy.

'There is of course a strong probability that I might be responsible,' he said in a firm voice.

'Oh yes, very strong.'

'In that case it is only reasonable that I should accept the responsibility.'

'Heavens above, if things really went as wrong as all that, all you'd have to do would be to pay a small sum for maintenance.'

'A sum for maintenance ... '

'Yes. And I should have to be paid my full salary for three months before and three months after the birth.'

'Your full salary ... '

'Yes. That's how things are arranged nowadays. On top of my salary I get free baby clothes, a pram, and six months' milk money, which can be exchanged anywhere for a case of beer. So what is there to get upset about?'

'A case of beer ... '

'Yes, and there are crèches and children's homes and kindergartens and I don't know what all. Everything is arranged beforehand, so there's no need to worry.'

'But Pernille, the child ... ?'

Pernille was so astounded at the Count's bewilderment and at the disappointment on his face that she suddenly began to think again, bit her lip in vexation, and said quickly: 'But if you are contemplating marriage with me, then of course the whole thing is quite different.'

Count Frederick told the story to Engelsen, and did not even attempt to hide his misery at finding his dream of love reduced to a matter between The Association for Helping Unmarried Mothers and his beloved, whom he was no longer sure he loved so very much after all.

Engelsen became extremely agitated, rated Pernille soundly, and told her that if she toyed with the idea of marriage he would speak to Count Hector and see to it that she was instantly dismissed.

'But why can't I marry Pernille?' asked Count Frederick, even while recognizing that it was mostly natural cussedness that made him say it. 'Isn't she my equal after all?'

Engelsen thought carefully before he answered.

'Yes, she is, my boy, but there are many kinds of equality

and some kinds are better than others. You and Pernille are not equal in the same way, if I may so express it. All animals are equal — but dogs and cats do not mate, do they?'

'Are you sure, dear Mr Engelsen, that your opposition does not spring from the fact that you would then have to give up your share in Pernille?'

'How can you be so reactionary?' said Engelsen hotly. 'No person ought to have any right of ownership over another. If that sort of thing still exists, it will soon be changed if only we are all sufficiently progressive. The share that we, and apparently a good many other people, have in Pernille's well-rounded liberality only goes to show how progressive we are in this country. Let us not confuse the issue.'

Count Frederick, however, continued to be just as confused, and he could not help feeling that somehow or other he was not quite at one with his tutor in his view of love.

CHAPTER TWO

*Count Frederick inherits
Egeborg and a Nationalization
Commission arrives.*

T HE year Count Frederick became a university student
Count Hector died. When he felt that the end was near,
he sent for his grandson and gave him the keys of the safe,
together with the name of a lawyer who never did business
with real estate companies and whose list of clients inspired
confidence. Then he blew his nose thoroughly and closed
his eyes.

'Aren't I going to have some good advice to help me on
my way?' asked Count Frederick.

Annoyed by this interruption, Count Hector answered:
'I have already given you three good rules. That is quite
enough. It is impossible to remember or to keep any more.'

'Have you yourself been able to live according to these
rules?'

'Asch! Of course not. One can never make more than
a good try at living as one should.'

'Supposing one had a try at one thing above all others,'
said Count Frederick. 'How would that be?'

Count Hector opened his eyes and looked a little more
favourably on his grandson.

'You're an obstinate fellow,' he said. 'That's good. One can
do almost anything one wants to do, as long as one does it.
As for whether there is one thing to be aimed at above all

others, hm! my answer is: see to it that you are always in love.'

Count Frederick thought with a certain melancholy of Pernille's melons, which he now regarded with businesslike, rather than loving, interest.

Count Hector grunted, and went on:

'It doesn't have to be women. A man can very well be in love with truth or prize cows or stocks and shares — it's not all that important. What matters is being in love.'

Count Hector's nose gave a final twitch, casting a gleam of roguishness over his transfigured countenance. 'If you want to go in for loving women, then that is one good reason for never marrying.' After a little he added: 'Unless you find a woman who understands that a man must always be in love one way or another.'

With a final neigh, and with the roguish expression still on his face, he gave up the ghost.

Some time after the funeral an official Nationalization Commission arrived. Its chairman, Mr Phrederickh Phrederickhsen, said that according to law half of all the land belonging to the castle must be turned into smallholdings. The commission consisted of twenty very fat men who were all extremely amiable while they were eating their lunch.

'The output of all the smallholdings together will be much less than that of the land today,' Count Frederick pointed out.

'It is impossible to prove that in advance,' said the chairman.

'The experience of past nationalizations is enough,' said the Count.

'One must not cling to past experience,' answered the chairman. 'It only confuses the issue.'

Count Frederick made no answer to this statement, for it was exactly what Engelsen had always said and so of course it must be right. But he informed the commission that the land left over for the castle's use, which was by far the smallest portion, would not be enough to carry running expenses. The castle's farming was bound to show a loss.

'Then you will get off paying taxes,' said the chairman encouragingly, 'so we are really doing you a service. Besides, it is not good for the community to allow too great a difference in profits; it only fosters discontent and ill-humour.'

After lunch the commission set off for the beach, where they all bathed to cool down their over-heated stomachs. They went into raptures over the beauty of the place, and agreed to requisition the beach and the plantation behind it so that city dwellers might have a much-needed breathing-space. The buttonhole in Mr Phrederickh Phrederickhsen's lapel would thus stand a very real chance of acquiring a decoration in recognition of his public-spiritedness.

Count Frederick did not raise any objection, for Engelsen had fully anticipated this too.

'Furthermore, this project will relieve the consciences of the members of the commission very considerably,' said Phrederickh Phrederickhsen jovially. 'Most of us have private bathing-beaches already, which is obviously a social injustice — but what can we do? We can't very well turn them into small breathing-spaces ourselves, can we?'

'Why not?'

'Ha, ha, ha! The Count is very amusing,' said Phrederickh Phrederickhsen. 'But that would make a proper mess of

things, whereas we do everything in an orderly fashion. With the nationalization of Egeborg beach we shall adjust the uneven balance which at present characterizes the division of nature's blessings.'

'So it is all quite all right, isn't it?' the Count asked Engelsen.

Engelsen had grown very pale, for he was fond of lying alone — or almost alone — on Egeborg beach; but he was a great idealist, so he replied: 'Yes, Count, and we ought to rejoice over all the pleasure we are about to give to others.'

'And ignore all the discontent that will result?' asked Count Frederick.

He thought how people would ruin the beach, and also one another's Sundays, with red petticoats, ice-cream tubs, sandwich paper, portable radios, motor-cycles, tent-ropes, tins, cigarette stubs, empty bottles, tops of beer bottles, broken cups, tin buckets, hairpins, broken sunglasses, dog, cat and other messes, old combs, empty cigarette packets, broken chair legs, torn bathing trunks, contraceptives, nail scissors, boxes, shoes, tin soldiers, shovels, spades, rakes, splintered oars, used gauze bandages, sticking plaster, nail-clippings, drinking straws, salt and pepper sprinklers, cats' eyes, repair kits, oil cans, daily papers, weekly papers, wrapping paper, cardboard boxes, gramophone needles, sanitary towels, punctured balls, rusty nails, drawing pins, forks, knives, spoons, food boxes, brassières, buttons, hand-kerchiefs, bats, sacks, old bits of carpet, pipes, pipe-cleaners, cigarette lighters, pocket books, pencils, chalk, ball-point pens, matches, primus stoves, saucepans, frying pans, water pistols, catapults, sheath-knives, driving licences, playing cards, maps, belts, teats, babies' nappies, toilet paper, withered flowers, lipsticks, powderpuffs, bathing wraps, suspenders, and vomit.

'One should not draw analogies between oneself and others when one is discussing the good of the community,' said Engelsen. 'The two have nothing whatever to do with each other.'

'But,' persisted Count Frederick, 'from a purely quantitative point of view the community must consist of the number of individuals comprising it.'

'There you make a mistake, my boy. As soon as even two people are gathered together, something exists above and beyond just those two. They form a whole, and the pleasures we as individuals have to sacrifice for the sake of the whole are repaid to us tenfold. *Ipso facto*, the more we offer of ourselves to the greater good, the more we receive from it, and when we have offered ourselves entirely we shall all become boundlessly rich and happy.'

'All of us?'

'Yes, all of us.'

The nationalization of Egeborg's land was quickly carried through, and the following summer the stream of motor-driven bicycles, motor-cycles, pedal cycles, cars, lorries and bubble cars rapidly increased.

The corn on the nationalized farms and in the fields of Egeborg itself became so trampled down that it was necessary to erect barbed wire round the fields at a cost of around five hundred pounds. There was no fruit harvest that year, since the emancipated holidaymakers pilfered very thoroughly. The cows gave less milk because some of the young people found great amusement in organizing home-made safaris on the animals, who were already very nervous. Owing to the many cases of injured feet a Red Cross station had to be set up; a police-station was built, and a police-sergeant and ten constables were appointed to keep the whole place in order, as well as two life-guards who were kept especially busy on days when the red flag was hoisted to show that bathing was forbidden. The rescued were put in the cells in the police-station and were later taken to the nearest court and fined.

About four or five hundred illegal pre-fabs suddenly sprang up on the estate and on the sand dunes, and as there was soon insufficient space, they encroached on some of the fields where the corn had already been so trampled down that it could no longer be harvested. Hundreds of ice-cream stalls also sprang up, together with souvenir shops, shacks selling antiques and bathing requisites and motors for bicycles, and bicycle repair shops. Three petrol stations were built, one car-repairing garage, one boat-builder's yard, and five pubs. For reasons unknown, only four of the pubs were licensed; consequently the fifth could not make good, so it sold smuggled spirits and set up a speakeasy, and in due course the proprietor and a number of people were arrested and given long prison sentences. A rich and varied crop of lawsuits took up most of the time of the local courts, as innumerable quarrels arose about rights of way, illegal shifting of boundaries, and smoke nuisance, in addition to a number of cases of rape, theft, burglary in week-end cottages, and parking offences. The rest of the plantation had to be made into a car park because, owing to the lack of stabilizing vegetation, the drifting sand had ruined a few hundred acres of farming land without anyone knowing who was to blame.

At the end of the summer all the pubs, ten of the shops, and all the filling stations, went bankrupt and had to be given a State subsidy. The municipality had to take up a big loan to adjust the drainage (there is no tide in the Baltic) so that it would be possible to bathe next year without being smeared all over with excrement. It would have been possible to get a grant from the money collected in tips to buy a sand-cleaning machine, but the 'Egeborg Lido' was forbidden to use it because there was considerable unemployment among the ice-cream sellers, innkeepers, waiters, garage attendants, life-guards, and supervisors of various kinds, and it would have been absurd to let a machine do work which would employ at least a hundred men with shovels and handpicks. However, this excellent idea was not at all popular among the unemployed. They would have preferred to pay for the machine out of the money they earned as sandcleaners and then let the machine do the work, while they drew almost their full wages for nothing more strenuous than watching the machine; which, after all, would have been tolerably amusing. But since it proved impossible to reach an agreement with the authorities, three more Red Cross posts had to be erected the following year to deal with feet that had been cut to pieces by the sort of things that are the natural consequences of civilization.

In order to finance all these projects the local rates had to be raised, which caused Egeborg to show a considerable loss. Furthermore, as the holidaymakers were upset to think that a count should be allowed to live alone in a castle and possess so much land while poor people on holiday had to crowd together in tents or in the car parks, an increasing amount of wanton destruction took place, directed at the castle buildings, the farm implements and the crops. No insurance company would agree to pay. Notices saying 'PRIVATE', 'NO ADMISSION' sparked off violent outbursts and battles with the castle staff. The two thousand five hundred dogs that came with the bathers chased the cows, sheep and horses, so that finally Egeborg was obliged to do away with all its livestock. Count Frederick no longer ventured outside the walls of the castle, for there were always a few hundred holidaymakers standing about waiting to stare at him, or climbing up the walls to look in at the windows. Often one of these inquisitive people fell down and broke a leg or an arm, when an action for damages was brought against the Count. These cost him considerable sums of money.

As most of the inhabitants of the tents, caravans, pre-fabs and week-end cottages had television, the new Landowners Association was able to forbid the castle farm to use its threshing machines when television programmes were on, as they spoiled the reception. Certain men were therefore appointed to thresh at night, of course at double overtime rates, but so many people declared that it disturbed their night's rest that this too had to be given up. Thus production came to a standstill. Nevertheless property taxes, rates, income and capital taxes had still to be paid. The Count therefore opened the castle to the public at a fee of 2s. 6d. a

head, which infuriated the left-wing press because of course it was preposterous that the public should not have free access to all the cultural blessings of their country.

As the visitors very soon destroyed all the furniture in the castle, Count Frederick at last decided to sell what remained to him. A trade union bought the castle and the surrounding land very cheaply. The State took over everything that was not covered by the purchase money and turned the castle into a conference house for trade union leaders.

With the exception of Engelsen and Pernille, whom the Count took with him to Copenhagen, the staff of the castle were given jobs as civil servants with fixed salaries and pensions, and the State voted a very large subsidy to put the castle in order and turn the surrounding fields into a park. The police-station was allotted a further ten men and two sergeants, so that definite action could now be taken against holidaymakers, who were no longer to be allowed to make free with public property. The whole of the 'Egeborg Lido' was highly organized and regulated, asphalted, signposted, managed, beautified with paths, public benches, look-out points, several car parks, and many communal litter baskets. Two unemployed barristers were appointed deputy judges to deal with all cases of violation of rules, regulations and by-laws, and two solicitors built up fat practices out of defending or accusing the patrons and the authorities respectively, as well as dealing with the many cases of bankruptcy which occurred every autumn due to the summer's unpaid bills.

The 'Egeborg Lido' became a model public breathing-space, where nature was so effectively superseded by modern culture that no one could have dreamt that Mr Engelsen and Pernille had lain there sunbathing in peaceful isolation, disturbed only by the shriek of the gulls and the soft laughter of the groundswell from a clean sea breaking on a white beach.

'It is wonderful what public welfare can accomplish,' said Engelsen, as he and Count Frederick and Pernille drove away from the gates of Egeborg for the last time.

Count Frederick did not reply.

CHAPTER THREE

*Count Frederick is instructed in the
excellency of the Housing Act, and
becomes a civil servant.*

COUNT FREDERICK had an old-fashioned flat with
thirteen rooms in one of the high-class, rather quieter
streets in the centre of Copenhagen. As he had nothing to
live on, and Engelsen and Pernille had nothing to live on
either, they decided to let rooms. This soon proved a very
profitable business, for the rent of the flat was controlled,
whereas the price of rooms was not, so that there was obviously a substantial margin of profit. Count Frederick was
rather surprised at this, but Engelsen explained that landlords could not be allowed to profit by the housing shortage.

'Is it better that the tenants should profit by it?' asked
Count Frederick.

'It is not pleasant to let rooms,' answered Engelsen, 'so
what could be more reasonable than that those who do
should get some compensation? It could not be better
arranged than it is, for the landlords get the bare minimum,
those who let rooms get an adequate payment for their
trouble, and those who want rooms get them.'

Their first lodger was a man named Pedersen who worked
in a State brewery. He was generally a very friendly man,
except on Sundays, when he always had a hangover.

'He is a good example,' said Engelsen, 'of the joy in work
that is found in State-owned concerns.'

The next room was let to a communist politician, Pellesen by name. He used it every Tuesday from four to six for going to bed with the wife of a ship-builder. This amused Engelsen very much and he said: 'What cannot be shared lawfully must be shared unlawfully. I am all for self-help in emergencies.'

The third and quietest room was used by a pools expert who had to have peace and quiet to work out his complicated permutations.

Finally, three rooms were let to a red-haired, powerful, rationalistic lady called Sonja Rasmussen. She had a mass-production technique. The first room was a waiting-room; in the second the clients were made ready for the production line by a lady assistant, and in the third the actual production took place.

The Count, his tutor and Pernille occupied the rest of the flat. It was not long, however, before the Count found a use for his inborn charm, Engelsen for his sense of diplomacy, and Pernille for her generosity. As Engelsen had very rightly predicted, the task of letting rooms proved both exacting and exhausting.

Pedersen, the brewery worker, disturbed the other lodgers on Sundays with loud complaints about his thirst, so that they were unable to sleep late in the mornings. Mr Pellesen's Tuesday arrangement was entirely spoilt because he could not keep his mind off Pernille, which was very distracting in circumstances where it would have been better for him to concentrate on what he had come for. The pools expert could not get the quiet he needed because of the continuous noise from Miss Sonja's room.

'It's the rhythm that gets me,' he explained, 'I can't leave off counting. I have a feeling for numbers, you see!'

The only one who was really content was Miss Sonja.

'This is such a nice, quiet street and these flats have such a discreet entrance,' she said. 'It convinces me that my profession is really highly valued by the general public.'

Unfortunately, the general public appreciated Miss Sonja's

merits more than did the Guardians of Society. One day a man turned up who introduced himself as Detective-Inspector Nammesen of the Public Morals Squad.

'Oh, good morning, Inspector,' said Engelsen. 'Please come in.'

The inspector looked at Engelsen with interest: 'Are you not the well-known scholar, Mr Engelsen?'

'That is not entirely incorrect.'

'As long as it is not entirely incorrect, dear sir, there is still hope. Unfortunately, I have to inform you that we suspect you and Count Frederick Christian Peder Wessel Ulrik-Ulrikkenfeldt of letting rooms for immoral purposes.'

'One should not be suspicious,' answered Engelsen.

'You are absolutely right,' said Nammesen, 'it is a tiresome human frailty, but what can one do about it?'

'One can try to see the best in everything.'

'You've got something there, but what do you suggest?'

'My dear Inspector, the Count's cousin is undoubtedly a lively young lady, but heavens above, you know what artists are.'

'That was a very optimistic explanation, I grant you,' answered Nammesen. 'You are a trusting sort of man, Mr Engelsen. Are you by any chance trying to tell me that Miss Sonja Rasmussen is not a lodger here?'

'A lodger!' Engelsen looked almost as if such a scandalous suggestion had caused him to lose ten pounds of fat from his cheeks. 'Do you think for a moment that the Count would take a penny piece from his cousin, that poor child who cannot find a room in the whole town on account of the housing shortage?'

'I should be reluctant to believe it of the Count.'

'So there we are.'

'There we are. But tell me what type of art she is interested in.'

'Miss Sonja is an acrobat.'

'Really? That sounds most interesting. But there are many forms of acrobatics, if I may say so.'

'Art is many-sided,' answered Engelsen.

'Undoubtedly. That sometimes makes it rather difficult for us to decide what is art and what is not. Perhaps you can help me.'

'As long as there is any doubt, it should be considered as art until it is proved that it isn't.'

'Excellent, Mr Tutor. You are helping me a great deal in my work.'

'Nothing could give me greater pleasure.'

'I believe you. But allow me to ask one more question. Why does this particular type of art require so many male visitors?'

As Engelsen hesitated a little before answering, Nammesen went on: 'Perhaps Miss Sonja has to take pupils to make any sort of living from her art?'

'Exactly. Artists' circumstances are often straitened.'

'True enough, but there is just one point that is still a little difficult,' said Nammesen. 'Why is it that the visitors are so often elderly men who scarcely seem adapted to acrobatic exercises?'

'You don't need much imagination to find the answer to that one,' answered Engelsen.

'Possibly not. I take it you have the necessary imagination?'

'You realize, I am sure,' explained Engelsen, 'that artists often have to compromise in order to stay alive — isn't that so?'

'Alas, yes. It is very sad,' said Nammesen.

'Miss Sonja, therefore, although she does not care for it, is obliged to teach remedial exercises.'

'Excellent,' said Nammesen. 'This will be a very satisfactory report. Have I expressed myself clearly enough?'

'It could not be put more clearly.'

'It could be,' said Nammesen, 'but we must hope for the best.'

'One should always hope for the best.'

'It will be the cheapest at any rate,' said Nammesen. 'Goodbye, and thank you.'

When Nammesen had gone, Count Frederick said: 'But what we are doing is illegal, and surely what is illegal must be detrimental to the general good?'

Engelsen answered: 'The interpretation of the law is extremely tricky. One should not always keep to the letter of the law; one should interpret the spirit and apply it accordingly, and not everybody is capable of doing this. If we took a higher rent from Miss Sonja than from the others, we should certainly not be interpreting the spirit of the law. But do we do that? Of course we don't. We are really showing an exceptionally strong social conscience in asking such a moderate rent when the temptation and opportunity to get a much higher one are so great. A man who has never been tempted cannot easily be moral. It is even more difficult for the man who is tempted, but if he does not yield, he is more highly moral than anyone else. So you and I are highly moral as well as highly social, my boy.'

'It is wonderful how well everything is arranged,' answered Count Frederick. 'The only pity is that as a rule one has to have someone explain it before it becomes clear.'

Meanwhile the problems with the other lodgers still remained to be solved, but here too Engelsen managed to arrange things. He lent Pernille to Mr Pellesen, the communist politician, every Tuesday from four to six, while he himself took charge of the ship-builder's wife.

'In this way we have managed to dispense with any payment to the middle-man,' he said, enchanted.

In return for the service that the Count and Engelsen had done Miss Sonja, it was arranged that the pools expert should be given a free treatment whenever the rhythm got on his nerves to such an extent that he could not work. And finally, they all agreed to club together for a case of beer to be put outside Pedersen's door every Sunday morning.

So peace and happiness reigned in the flat. But this prompted Engelsen to say that it was not a good thing for a young man like Count Frederick to have so much free time on his hands; so in spite of the fact that they lived very comfortably on the rents from the rooms, he obtained, with the help of his political friends, a position for the Count in the Foreign Office in the Department for Cultural Exchanges with Friendly Nations.

On the day Count Frederick began work in the Department for Cultural Exchanges he knocked at a door marked 'Mr Ming — Section Manager'.

'Come in,' came the answer.

Count Frederick entered a large, light room in which there was nothing except a desk with Mr Ming behind it. There were no papers of any kind anywhere to be seen and nothing on the desk except Mr Ming's own well-manicured hands. Count Frederick introduced himself and Mr Ming rose and said: 'To what do I owe this honour?'

Count Frederick was somewhat taken aback by the friendliness of Ming's voice, for his face was completely impassive — which seemed strange, seeing that it was so long and so much needed a little animation. Ming was very tall, very pale, and dressed in black.

'I am supposed to begin work here today,' said Count Frederick.

'Really? Well, that's up to you. If you would prefer another day, that will be perfectly all right.'

'I don't think you have quite understood me,' said Count Frederick. 'My appointment is from today and I am to receive a salary from today.'

'I am delighted on your account,' said Mr Ming, 'but that does not mean that you need necessarily start work today.'

'Would it not be best to do so?'

'That depends entirely on how you look at it, Count.'

'I haven't the slightest objection to starting work today.'

'None at all? Not the least little bit?'

'No, none at all.'

'How different people can be,' sighed Mr Ming. 'Are you absolutely certain that you would not prefer to begin tomorrow or some other day?'

'Absolutely certain — unless you have anything against it.'

'Don't ask me,' answered Mr Ming, lifting his hands to ward off the question. 'I have problems enough already.'

'Then I should prefer to start today.'

'All right, all right, if you absolutely insist on it. Is there anything special you would like to do?'

'I should like to do whatever you want me to do.'

'You're not being very helpful, Count.'

'I'm sorry.'

'Don't mention it. H'm. Let me see, then we must find something to interest you.'

'Thank you.'

'Thank *you*. Shall we go this way, if it suits you?'

Mr Ming took Frederick into a room where foreign newspapers and journals were stacked on shelves reaching from floor to ceiling.

'Could you bring yourself to clip out any articles concerning Denmark you can find in these papers?'

'Certainly.'

'Can you really bring yourself to do it?' asked Ming, quite amazed. 'Very well: if you are absolutely certain, there you are.'

'I suppose the articles will have to be catalogued eventually?' asked Count Frederick.

'Catalogued? Yes, yes of course, they will have to be catalogued. What would you suggest?'

'They could be divided into two groups. Friendly and unfriendly.'

'Excellent, Count, excellent, so long as you do not think it would be too much trouble.'

'Not at all. Perhaps, however, it might be better to make a more detailed classification. For example, one could distinguish between: excessively laudatory, very laudatory, very friendly, friendly, sober, truthful, less friendly, not at all friendly, positively hostile, abusive, lying, scandalous, and nationally provocative.'

Frederick was very anxious to make a good impression.

Mr Ming's horselike face seemed to tremble a little, but that might have been the bad light in the archive room.

'You really must not overwork yourself, Count,' he said, and departed hastily.

Frederick, who was not a little proud of having become a civil servant, and in the Foreign Office too, began snipping and clipping as if his life depended on it. However, he realized immediately that it would be impossible for him to carry out the work alone and he therefore asked Ming for some assistance.

'I thought as much,' replied Ming obligingly. 'It has been too much for you. How about a little leave?'

'Certainly not. I find the work very interesting, but is there no one in the office who can be spared?'

'Spared? Yes, of course, Count. Let me see, let me see. There are ten clerical assistants, two secretaries, one chief clerk and one permanent under-secretary all sitting in Room Five who can well be spared, if that would be enough for you.'

'Many thanks, that is far too much.'

'Not at all, not at all. Say no more about it.'

Careful statistics were now worked out of the number of articles in each category, the lengths of the columns, and the possible connection between these and the time of year, particular political conditions, royal visits, economic trends, fluctuations in agricultural prices, number of tourists, and so on. A distinction was also made between those writers who had never been to Denmark and those who had. As was expected, the first group was by far the larger.

Frederick soon discovered that unfortunately he was

tremendously unpopular with the staff in Room Five, although he could not understand why. However, he did his best, and he was full of new ideas, whose implementation in due course required a further ten clerical assistants, two secretaries, a chief clerk and an under-secretary. Ming called him in and asked him urgently whether he did not think that he now needed a little leave. When Frederick denied it in the strongest terms, Ming said:

'Then I shall be obliged to get myself appointed Head of the Department, for I can see that we shall need many more section managers — my present grade. Are you quite sure that a little leave ... ?'

'Yes, sir, quite, quite sure.'

Mr Ming was therefore appointed Head of the Department and two new section managers took over his work. Because of the increased staff, Count Frederick suggested that a personnel office should be established, to which Ming agreed with a sick look at Frederick's still excited face. The personnel office looked after the civil servants' salaries, housing, income tax arrears, alimony, divorce costs, superannuation, loan fund, and insurance premiums. This swelling administration brought about a certain amount of political criticism, after which an Investigating Committee was appointed, consisting of ten specialists, who concluded that the Department for Cultural Exchanges with Friendly Nations ought to be given the status of a Ministry. This suited the existing Government admirably, since some ministers were still without portfolio. In the course of all this development Count Frederick advanced rapidly to the position of section manager. Later he was given a ministerial secretaryship, which meant that he had his own secretariat with a section manager of his own, two under-secretaries, four chief clerks, eight secretaries, and about fifty clerical assistants, only half of whom were generally present as the other half were out attending meetings, at lunch, having coffee- and tea-breaks, and visiting the lavatory.

Count Frederick kept Engelsen informed of everything

that happened in the rapidly expanding Ministry for Cultural Exchanges, and as it quickly became apparent that the building where they were working was quite inadequate, Engelsen suggested that Count Frederick should send in a memorandum detailing the many advantages that would accrue if the Ministry bought Egeborg Castle for the use of the said administration.

'We shall thus get back to where we belong,' said Engelsen. 'The lovely castle will be used for a worthy purpose and the Ministry be housed in suitable surroundings.'

Count Frederick nodded, but thought it a very costly and roundabout way of getting back to his ancestral home.

'What do the means matter as long as the end is right?' answered Engelsen. 'Something must be sacrificed if everyone is to be satisfied, and one must not be narrow-minded. This development only shows that the public good cannot but attain to the best of all possible results in the end.'

So Egeborg Castle was bought for a very large sum and practically rebuilt, so that it looked exactly as it had done in the days when the Ulrikkenfeldt family lived in it. It was to house a Cultural Institution, after all. The public breathing-space known as 'Egeborg Lido' was closed to all unauthorized persons, for it was important to make a good impression on foreign guests. The expropriation payments for all the summer cottages and car parks, football grounds, shops, factories and storehouses ran into many thousands of pounds, but on the other hand no one could now remain in doubt of the very high cultural standing of the country.

A number of notices were posted up with the following words: '*No admission except to authorized persons. Trespassers will be prosecuted under Paragraph No. 323456 of the Act of May 3rd, 1945. See Note to Act No. 456 of October 23rd, 1923. See Act No. 57 of March 26th, 1918.*'

Right up to the moment of the actual moving of the extensive archives and the enormous card index, Count Frederick felt full of social energy and showed a growing inclination to share Engelsen's enthusiasm for public welfare.

The move changed all that. A member of parliament thought it would be too expensive to use lorries for the transport of the files, and as there were currently a great many un-employed, to say nothing of students who wanted to earn money during the vacation, it was decided that all documents should be transported on tricycles. It was a very hot day, and when the procession was passing over a bridge, Mr Ming halted it and suggested a rest. Ming's glance wandered once or twice from the bundles of papers in the sidecars to the water below, and at length he said to Count Frederick:

'Why not pitch half the archives into the sea? It would make things easier for the cyclists.'

'But it represents several years' work,' exclaimed Count Frederick, aghast.

'Does it really? Then it's more than time that it was weeded out. All those records must distract your soaring ideas. Besides, no one will miss them. And think how pleased the Investigation Committee will be.'

So several hundredweights of documents were dumped in the sea and the procession continued towards Egeborg at a distinctly quicker pace. Count Frederick, however, was deeply disappointed and complained to Engelsen of the entire absence of a sense of values in the Welfare State.

'You are making a mistake, my boy,' said Engelsen. 'Think how much more effectively the Ministry can now work, how many more staff have been appointed, and how lovely Egeborg has become again. You really must not judge progress by the loss of a few dirty bits of paper.'

'I think on the whole I prefer to let rooms,' said the Count.

CHAPTER FOUR

Count Frederick and Engelsen reach Moscow as members of a delegation. The Count has an experience of an amorous nature on Marxist-Leninist principles.

W HEN the half of the files and archives which had not been dumped in the sea had been safely stored away in the cellars of Egeborg, Count Frederick sat down at his desk, which he now took care to keep absolutely clear of papers, and placed his well-manicured hands on its shining surface. He did this every day for a long time and it made him very popular indeed.

One day Ming said to him:

'My dear Count, now that you are quite at home with our methods in the Ministry for Cultural Exchanges with Friendly Nations, and have thoroughly absorbed the most fundamental of all administrative laws, namely, "something unaccomplished, something done", the Minister is considering offering you a very important post — unless, of course, you have any objection.'

Now, although Count Frederick had been deeply disillusioned at an early age with regard to love, the nationalization of his estate, the housing laws, and the general value of statistical investigations, he yet retained an enthusiastic and zealous glint in his blue eyes. Besides, he was always aware that he might be misunderstanding the world, and that, as Engelsen had explained to him, it was in reality much better than it appeared. He therefore gave Mr Ming an encouraging nod.

'We wondered,' Mr Ming continued, 'whether you would care to lead a delegation to the Soviet Union, and as we have had the opportunity here in Egeborg of becoming acquainted with your servant Mr Engelsen, we should be very pleased if you would take him along with you. As far as I know, such a journey would agree perfectly with his political ideas, and I believe he can also speak Russian, which would be ideal because you would then have a ready-made interpreter with you.'

'It will be a pleasure,' said Count Frederick, bowing.

'It is a pleasure that you are prepared to undertake this mission,' said Mr Ming, and he too bowed.

'I shall be sorry to leave the Ministry,' said the Count with another bow.

'We shall be very sorry to lose you,' said Mr Ming, bowing in return.

'But I shall soon be back,' said the Count. He bowed low.

'No hurry, no hurry at all, my dear Count,' said Mr Ming, bowing yet again.

Engelsen was overjoyed at the prospect of the trip.

'Now we shall be able to see what the world looks like when it has become the best of all worlds,' he cried.

But Pernille sulked.

'Hasn't either of you thought how much you will miss me? Who will see that you have clean shirts every morning, who will find your studs, see that your fly-buttons are properly fastened, brush the hairs off your shoulders, see that Engelsen has his beer openers and corkscrews in his brief-case, open the caviar, oil the springs of the bed so that they don't creak, sew buttons on your pyjamas, buy tooth-brushes, press your trousers, have the cold whisky and sodas ready for you when you have been talking too much, and warm you up when you are cold?'

'There's something in that,' said Engelsen, and the Count decided there and then to write a memorandum to the Ministry under the following heading: '*Considerations affecting the necessity for Miss Pernille's inclusion in the Delegation to be sent to the Soviet Union by the Ministry for Cultural Exchanges with Friendly Nations.*'

The application was granted and Pernille immediately began to pack trunks, while Engelsen worked energetically collecting the names of Russian dishes that he wanted to

sample. Count Frederick used the days before their departure for studying some of the places and things of interest

that the Russians were
likely to show the dele-
gation. He soon realized
that it was an enormous
task, for to get a true
picture of modern Russia
one would have to
visit the world's lar-
gest underground
railway station, the
world's greatest
dam, the world's
longest railway line,
the world's cham-
pion milch cow, the world's strongest woman, largest statue,
hugest university; besides that, he would have to visit the
inventors of the aeroplane, car and motor-cycle, the atomic
theory, the parachute, the hydrogen bomb, the tommy-gun,
the film, the telephone, the tram, the shot through the back
of the head, the concentration camp, the reinterpretation of
history, embalming, quintuple-yielding rye, jamming radio
stations, brainwashing, public confession, space travel, and
truth drugs.

'Let us stick to caviar and vodka, and for the rest content
ourselves with rejoicing over the joys of the Russian people,'
said Engelsen. 'That will be experience enough for us.'

On the day of departure the members of the delegation
met at the airport, and great was the joy when they recognized as one of their members the communist politician,
Pellesen, with whom Engelsen, Pernille and the ship-builder's
wife had in the past had a quadripartite agreement that had
worked perfectly. Another was the chairman of the
Nationalization Commission that had originally done so
much for public welfare when Egeborg was taken over by
the State.

Count Frederick, who was always courteous, said: 'I am delighted to meet you again.'

Mr Phrederickh Phrederickhsen answered that he was always delighted to meet anyone who was delighted to meet him.

The third was the author Ole Windbagsen, editor of an independent cultural journal dedicated to telling the truth about the Soviet Union. The fourth was Professor Friede, a very friendly and quite colourless man. And the fifth was none other than Pedersen the brewery worker.

They soon made friends all round and agreed that the turbo-jet that the Russians had sent to fetch them was the largest and loveliest plane they had ever seen. Unfortunately it was not possible to talk much during the journey because of the tremendous roar of the engines in the cabin, but Engelsen said that one could not expect anything else from so large and speedy a machine, and that it was reassuring to hear the engines all the time as one could then be sure that there was nothing wrong with them. The five members of the delegation were unanimous in their agreement on this point.

When they landed at Moscow aerodrome they were received by a guard of honour with fixed bayonets, and a company of N.K.V.D. police, with all of whom the delegates were expected to shake hands very cordially. Count Frederick thought the secret police seemed particularly interested in pressing the visitors' hands while they stared fixedly at their faces. Engelsen said: 'How charming they are.'

Pedersen proclaimed in Russian to all the N.K.V.D. men: 'I have come to study Soviet beer.' It was the only thing he could say in Russian, but it certainly sounded very convincing.

Pernille gazed entranced at the soldiers' bayonets, and when finally she was introduced to the Russian who was to act as contact man to the delegation during their visit she said to him: 'I have never seen better kitchen knives. I should like to take one of those home with me.'

The contact man, who had told them that his name was
Batjusjov, laughed unrestrainedly and, kissing Pernille on
both cheeks, answered: 'Nothing could be easier, my child,
and from this the Western dollar-capitalist war-debauched
world may learn that the Soviet Union is the most peaceful
of all nations, for even our bayonets are in reality only
kitchen knives.'

'I have come to study Soviet beer,' said Pedersen, and at
this Comrade Batjusjov laughed more heartily still and
thumped the Dane violently on the back. 'Nothing could be
easier, my friend, and from this the Western dollar-capitalist
war-debauched world may learn that here in the Soviet
Union one does not swill beer as one does in the drunken
West, one *studies* it.'

The author Ole Windbagsen said that he had come to write
the truth about the Soviet Union. 'Nothing could be easier,'
answered Batjusjov, 'for in the Soviet Union everything is
true, and in fact a great many things are particularly true.'

The communist politician, Mr Pellesen, said that he was

looking forward to meeting his fellow party-members. 'Nothing is easier,' answered Batjusjov.

'I believe you,' said Count Frederick, 'for here I suppose everybody is a party-member.'

'Almost everybody.'

'Then it is not a particular truth that everybody is?'

'No,' answered Batjusjov, 'it is only a truth.'

Mr Phrederickh Phrederickhsen said that he was looking forward to seeing a collective farm.

To this Batjusjov made no answer.

Professor Friede said nothing at all.

Engelsen, on the other hand, said a great deal in Russian. At first Batjusjov looked at him suspiciously, then he exhibited an ever-increasing amazement and confusion. 'Forgive me,' he said in Danish, 'but I do not understand what you are saying.'

Engelsen spoke louder and more quickly and gesticulated eagerly, but Batjusjov shook his head.

'You speak a very melodious language with a very rich vocabulary,' he said, 'but I do not know it. Can't you speak Danish?'

'Yes, of course, but this is Russian,' answered Engelsen.

'Is it really? Then it must be a dialect that I have never heard before,' answered Batjusjov. 'Will you allow me to give you some good advice? Stick to Danish. That is *very* good advice, Mr Engelsen.'

Engelsen was deeply disappointed, but a little later he cheered up and said to Count Frederick: 'Of course — now I've got it. Comrade Batjusjov was understandably vexed at having a rival interpreter, seeing that he himself is so anxi ι s to speak Danish. What a charming way of indicating it.'

'Very charming,' said the Count.

A long cortège of black cars awaited them outside the airport.

'It is strange how much they resemble my father's Packard,' said Count Frederick. 'But that is probably only a truth and not a particular truth.'

'One should not always judge by outward appearances,' said Engelsen.

The delegates were placed singly in the back and front seats respectively of the different cars, each one between two N.K.V.D. men, and the cortège drove off into the town at breakneck speed with horns blaring and brakes screeching.

'Could we not drive a little more slowly,' suggested Count Frederick.

'Unfortunately not,' answered Batjusjov. 'There are so many cars on the streets of Moscow that everyone has to drive very fast to keep the traffic moving.'

Count Frederick thought the streets seemed fairly empty, but that was no doubt because they were driving so fast.

The delegates were installed at the Hotel Balaclava, which had been so named after Russia's victory in the Crimean War. The hotel décor was exactly like a hotel décor during that same Crimean War.

'What veneration for history,' said Engelsen.

They had a meal immediately and ate caviar and drank vodka. Pedersen said that he had come to study Soviet beer but there was no reason why he should not enlarge his field of study and include vodka.

Batjusjov saw to it that Pedersen drank a large amount of vodka in a very short time, after which he asked him to sign a document stating that the well-known beer expert, Comrade Pedersen from Denmark, herewith testified that Soviet beer was the best in the world.

'Beer or vodka,' said Pedersen, 'the effects are obviously the same, and they are every bit as good as they are at home.'

Then he signed with large capital letters and added under his name: '*Student-in-the-Soviet-Beer-Delegation*'.

The author Ole Windbagsen noted in his journal that in the Soviet Union one ate caviar and drank vodka at every meal, and that a large number of the hotels were museums as well as hotels.

The communist politician Comrade Pellesen whispered

excitedly to Comrade Batjusjov as they took turns in pinching Pernille's two lower melons.

Pernille went on eating caviar and did not allow herself to be distracted.

Mr Phrederickh Phrederickhsen continued to shout across the table to Batjusjov that he was looking forward to seeing a collective farm. Batjusjov answered by lifting his glass and shouting, 'Skaal.'

Professor Friede said nothing.

Engelsen did not say anything either, for at this juncture there was no room in his mouth for words because he was carrying out a number of interesting experiments which consisted in combining varying amounts of caviar and vodka. Although his mouth was very large, his taste organs were particularly fine and it was amazing how many possible combinations there were. The difficulty with the experiments was soon apparent, however, for there were several different quantity-combinations which produced results of equal quality, and this was extremely confusing and unsatisfactory to a brain as clear as Engelsen's.

Nevertheless he succeeded at last in advancing to a point where he could assert, with some degree of certainty, that two parts caviar to one part vodka was the most attractive combination. He estimated the quantities as follows: one dessertspoonful of caviar to one half beer glass full of vodka per mouthful. He then leaned back in his chair, patted his stomach, and reflected that a round firm stomach was a very attractive thing, besides being pleasant to the touch. He looked round at the other members of the loud-voiced company to find one to whom he could communicate his present well-being, but everyone was very busy. In the course of this survey he received a sudden shock, for when he looked at Count Frederick he immediately became aware that something important was about to happen. A young woman whom he had not noticed before was sitting beside the Count. Despite her clumsy clothes, there was no doubt whatever but that she was singularly shapely.

This fact could calmly be reckoned among the particular truths.

Vera Kovalof had arrived some time after the party had begun, so she gave up the idea of introducing herself all round, and, after studying the delegates, decided to go and sit beside Count Frederick. This greatly pleased the Count, who was feeling a little lonely. His pleasure was not in any way decreased after he had studied her more closely. It was true that her bright hair — like the sun on an early June morning — was drawn back with mathematical precision into a tight bun at the nape of her neck, that she hid her delights under a military-style blouse made of coarse cotton and a thick brown nether garment, and that she wore broad flat shoes which did not seem to differentiate between the right foot and the left, but there was no need to be a great connoisseur to see that her swan neck moved gracefully, that her breasts were set close together and were in a state of constant uplift, that her waist was idyllic and soft to embrace, that the generous breadth of her hips would easily withstand great weights and much violence, and that her legs held the same potentiality for girlish enjoyment as do cats' paws when they stretch luxuriously. However, her strong face, with its straight nose and powerful cheekbones, expressed only diplomatic and polite interest, and her voice sounded as if she were trying to speak unnaturally correctly. She informed Count Frederick that she was the hostess to the delegation and would also act as interpreter if Comrade Batjusjov were engaged.

In all serious situations Count Frederick was apt to remember his grandfather's advice that, among other things, one should always tell the truth. He therefore said that she was the loveliest woman he had ever seen and that he was already in love with her.

Vera Kovalof looked at him first in a puzzled sort of way and then gave a forced laugh. 'The Danes have such a strange sense of humour,' she said. 'Danish culture is my special subject at the university, and I have been studying

Danish humour for a whole term, but it is very difficult to find examples of humour in your literature unless one has been told beforehand which bits are funny. I suppose it is a joke when you tell me that you are in love with me?'

'No, that is not a joke.'

Vera Kovalof shook her Tolstoyan head in despair. 'I don't understand it,' she said.

'It was meant seriously,' said the Count.

This time Vera Kovalof laughed in earnest. 'Now you are really being funny.'

'Why is that so funny?'

'Because love is a very serious matter indeed, which can only be decided when two people know each other to be entirely faithful to the Party and to the Soviet Union, and when the unit to which they belong has decided that marriage would be useful in their work.'

'I cannot see that those things have anything to do with love.'

'There, you see, it *was* a joke. What you said did not apply at all, and therefore it was a joke.'

The Count bent forward hastily and kissed her.

Vera Kovalof's lips were cold and flabby from surprise. Then she pushed him away violently. 'How dare you? You are a degenerate, decadent representative of the decaying West.'

'Your mouth, Comrade Delegation-hostess Vera Kovalof, is like a giant poppy in a newly mown lawn,' he said, sighing deeply. 'But I am not certain that you have quite understood your duties as hostess,' he added. 'At any rate your studies of Danish culture have not given you any great understanding of our way of life. I think I shall complain to Comrade Batjusjov about you.'

'How can you be so horrible,' cried Vera Kovalof, terror-stricken.

'You are mistaken,' answered the Count. 'I was only trying to help you with your studies of the Danish attitude to life. Tell me, is it not the intention that you, as delegation hostess, should see to it that your guests are as happy and comfortable as possible?'

She nodded.

'And a foreigner feels most comfortable when he is able to behave as he does at home. Isn't that so?'

She nodded.

'If you had been Danish you would have thrust your tongue into my mouth when I kissed you, asked me for the number of my room, and told me not to lock my door tonight.'

This time Vera Kovalof did not nod.

He went on: 'Is it the object of these cultural exchanges that we should instruct each other in the various customs in our respective countries?'

She nodded again.

'As your studies obviously have not taught you very much about my nation, is it not high time that you filled the gaps in your knowledge by carefully carrying out those duties which your Party and the Soviet Union have entrusted to you — the duties of a hostess?'

'That is all right dialectically,' she answered, 'but I am obliged to let the higher authorities make the final decision.'

'Excellent,' said Count Frederick, 'I will wait for you.'

Vera Kovalof rose, drew Batjusjov aside and had a long conversation with him, after which Batjusjov disappeared and Vera Kovalof returned to the Count.

'The matter has been referred to the secretariat,' she said. 'In the meantime I should just like to know whether your suggestion is an expression of Danish humour or whether it forms part of the policy of reducing tension advocated by the Soviet Union — so far without result.'

'It is love pure and simple,' answered the Count, 'but since in all love there is not a little humour mixed in with the tension and its reduction, I think I can answer yes to both your questions.'

'So there is only an apparent contradiction between the two hypotheses,' answered Vera Kovalof, obviously relieved. 'In reality they are both absorbed into a higher unity.'

'Exactly,' answered the Count. 'You are not only lovely, but you are extremely intelligent. It is this higher unity towards which we must all strive. I am glad you are so well grounded in Hegel.'

'There is no beer in the world like Soviet beer,' shouted Pedersen to Professor Friede.

'Unfortunately I cannot express an opinion,' answered the Professor, 'for I have never tasted Soviet beer and I have only a comparatively slender acquaintance with the beers of other countries.'

'Nonsense, nonsense,' shouted Pedersen. 'Don't split hairs. One should not make a fuss over trifles.'

Engelsen lifted his glass to drink to Count Frederick and his table companion, and said that Vera Kovalof was conclusive evidence that when they were all equal the women were lovelier than ever, and it pleased him to see that his pupil had obviously realized the truth of this excellent theory.

'The effect is indisputable,' answered the Count, 'but whether you are right about the cause, Engelsen, is perhaps more doubtful.'

'Has Comrade Engelsen said something funny?' Vera whispered to the Count.

'Engelsen is always saying something funny,' he replied, and Vera gave herself up to energetic laughter.

'Have you ever seen such a gay and lovely girl?' asked Engelsen.

'No,' answered the Count.

'And the Soviet Union is built on principles of equality, is it not?'

'So it is said.'

'Ergo, beauty may be the result of equality. Correct?'

'Some of the waitresses are not particularly pretty,' the Count observed.

'My son,' sighed Engelsen, 'all beauty is subjective, and if the beauty of the waitresses has not impressed you it is only because you cannot see it. You are temporarily in a state

where you have eyes for Comrade Vera Kovalof's beauty
alone, but that does not prove that all the other women in
this country are not beautiful too, does it?'

'But are you not in the same state, Engelsen?'

'Of course not. I can see that all Soviet women are beautiful, but that does not prevent me from seeing that some are
more beautiful than others.'

'From the point of view of foreign policy, it would certainly be wiser to toast on the assumption that this contention is correct,' said the Count.

'It is not a contention,' answered Engelsen. 'It is an *a priori*
theory that is so obvious that it needs no verification.'

'Your health,' said the Count.

Ole Windbagsen had been gazing for a long time at Comrade Kovalof and he now took out his notebook and wrote
down: 'Soviet women are the most beautiful in the world.
For this reason they dress very simply because they do not
need to behave coquettishly to attract attention to their
beauty.'

Pernille had finally eaten enough caviar and was therefore
quite willing to allow herself to be distracted by Comrade
Batjusjov and Mr Pellesen.

Batjusjov rose and proposed a toast to Denmark.

The Count rose and proposed a toast to the Soviet Union.

Pedersen tried to rise to propose a toast to Soviet beer.

Phrederickh Phrederickhsen rose and proposed a toast to
Soviet State-controlled agriculture.

Batjusjov rose and proposed a toast to the collective farms.

Phrederickhsen rose and proposed a toast to Soviet State-
controlled agriculture.

Batjusjov rose and proposed a toast to the collective farms.

Professor Friede drank a toast all by himself.

Pellesen rose and proposed a toast to the Cominform, but
Batjusjov waved it aside, saying that they must first ask the
Politburo whether such a toast was in order.

Pellesen then suggested a toast to Tito instead, but Batjusjov
said that such a toast must also be gone into more carefully.

Then Pellesen tried, somewhat irritably, to propose a toast to a successful meeting of the Big Four in Geneva, but Batjusjov answered, equally irritably, that it would be better to close down on toasts.

Engelsen then suggested that they should drink to that resolution.

Pedersen was carried out by a strapping and subjectively pretty Soviet waitress.

Engelsen suggested that they should drink to the toast of 'No More Toasts.'

Batjusjov said that Engelsen was a great dialectician.

Professor Friede said that he was tired after the journey and wished to withdraw. Batjusjov clapped his hands and two strapping and subjectively pretty Soviet waitresses took the professor up to his room.

A member of the N.K.V.D. delivered two long official-looking documents to Batjusjov and to Comrade Vera Kovalof. The heading read: '*The secretariat's pronouncement regarding the duties and rights of Comrade Vera Kovalof, Soviet hostess to the delegation, in the matter of the appreciation of Danish humour, together with the policy of reducing tension between the Soviet Union and Denmark.*' First of all there was a great deal about the Marxist-Leninist principles on which one should act, and after that a number of more concrete paragraphs on how the particular couple should act. Comrade Vera Kovalof was in duty bound to spend one hour in Count Frederick's bedroom, and during this time she was to take part in one single act of copulation whose duration should not exceed twenty minutes and which should give her a thorough knowledge of Danish humour. It was naturally assumed that as a true Soviet woman and faithful party-member she would not give herself up to degenerate Western excesses and would confine herself strictly to the educational aspects of the matter.

Batjusjov read the document carefully, gazed for a long time at Pernille, and then asked the N.K.V.D. messenger to take a similar application to the secretariat on behalf of himself and Comrade Pernille. When Pellesen heard this he broke a bottle of vodka on Batjusjov's bald skull.

This angered Batjusjov, and Pellesen was forcibly removed by four N.K.V.D. men.

In the meantime another N.K.V.D. emissary had appeared beside Phrederickh Phrederickhsen and surreptitiously given him an injection. Then the man repeated to him: 'I am anxious to see a communal farm. I am anxious to see a communal farm. I am anxious to see a communal farm.' Before long Phrederickhsen willingly repeated the sentence, whereupon he also was carried out by a strapping and subjectively pretty Soviet waitress.

Engelsen himself carried out a subjectively pretty Soviet waitress.

Count Frederick kissed Comrade Vera Kovalof and she thrust her tongue into his mouth and asked the number of his room. After he had answered, she told him not to lock his door.

'It *is* amusing, isn't it?' she asked anxiously.

Count Frederick was not in a condition to answer as the sap was rising in him so violently that he had to hurry up to his room.

Vera Kovalof followed him quickly.

Comrade Batjusjov and Pernille remained behind, alone, waiting for the decision of the secretariat.

Vera Kovalof placed an alarm clock on Count Frederick's bedside table.

'It will go off in an hour's time.'

'Your eyes are like two pole stars,' he answered.

Vera Kovalof placed another alarm clock beside it.

'This one will ring twenty minutes after we have set it,' she announced.

'Your breasts are two nestlings, and my hands a nest,' he murmured.

'I hope you read the secretariat's statement very thoroughly,' she said.

The Count kissed her very thoroughly.

'Oh,' she said, 'Danish humour has such a strange effect on me.'

After that Count Frederick kissed Vera in many different places.

'Danish humour must be true humour,' she whispered, 'for I do not know whether to laugh or to cry and that is the effect true humour has, isn't it?'

After that neither of them spoke for a long time, and they forgot to set the twenty-minute alarm clock. When at last the other alarm clock went off Vera laughed and wept at the same time, stretched out her naked and perfect arm to stop the ringing, and said:

'Hegel is a great philosopher, and Danish humour is very exhausting.'

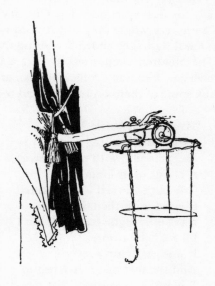

CHAPTER FIVE

Comrade Pedersen sings a Danish folk song to the dear little Soviet children. Count Frederick and Vera Kovalof are absorbed in love, while the members of the delegation disappear one by one.

Every evening when Pedersen had finished visiting Soviet breweries he was taken to a hospital where he was questioned, given an injection and put to bed, so that he might be ready for new visits next day. One day when they had been to a brewery where they had studied various types of beer from Kazakstan, they ended by visiting the children's playroom. The children clamoured to hear a Danish folk song, and Pedersen, who was a rollicking man and no mean musician, took some of them on his knee and began to sing:

'My dear old Uncle Matt
Enriched his ageing mind
Each evening with the *Decameron*,
A classic of its kind.
One page worked loose and fell.
I found it on the floor.
I was only eight years old, but I think
I'll see it evermore.
It was page thirty-seven,
And the text had scarce begun
When there occurred that naughty word
That the sailor said to the nun.'

After Pedersen had sung the first verse, Batjusjov translated as follows: 'The good old books such as we have here in the Soviet Union are not available in the war-debauched, dollar-capitalist, degenerate and corrupt West. Instead, there is a mass of indecent, horrible stuff which it is very undesirable for children to read. Nevertheless they are not only allowed to read it — they are actually forced to do so in the schools, although they do not like it. The song tells of an innocent little boy who was beaten unless he read a horrible book every evening which told what a filthy low-down nun forced an honest hard-working sailor to say.'

> 'The arguments wax fierce
> About those army brutes
> Who cause a lack of esprit de corps
> Between officers and recruits.
> When I joined up I was
> A gently nurtured boy.
> Alas that this was the very thing
> My sergeant should destroy!
> For great was my dismay,
> When the day had scarce begun,
> To hear him use that naughty word
> That the sailor said to the nun.'

'This verse tells us,' Batjusjov translated, 'that in the Danish army the officers are entirely horrible, as the aristocratic guards officers in the Czar's army used to be, and they beat the poor soldiers who are men of the people and have had to leave their work to slave for the king who exploits them and the country. When the little boy was old enough he had to be a soldier for ten years, and then the guards officers beat him, and kept shouting at him the wicked word that the horrible pope-crazy nun had forced the kind sailor to say.'

> 'An educational journal
> Advertised: "Canes for sale."

So there's no protection now for kids
However they weep and wail.
The first blow lately fell
When little Jens got fresh,
For the pliant rod came whistling down
And left its mark on the flesh.
Jens, red in the face with rage,
Though the beating had scarce begun,
Let slip that naughty word
That the sailor said to the nun.'

'In the Danish schools the children are caned every day if they do not fall on their knees whenever they pass the picture of the king with all his fat capitalists, who exploit the people and make cannons and hydrogen bombs with which to kill all of us peace-loving communists,' said Batjusjov. 'One day the darling little boy of whom we are speaking was caned until he bled by one of the king's lackeys because he had whispered to one of his companions that he was a communist and wanted to go to the Soviet Union if only he could escape from the slave camp which the whole of the Western world had become. And since, as you heard in the first verse, he had only read very bad books, he said aloud the frightful word that the horrible pope-crazy nun had forced on the sailor who was a Hero of Labour.'

'My dear old Uncle Matt —
Now you remember him! —
Saw an advert: "French teacher seeks a home",
And answered it on a whim.
A French teacher? My foot!
From the French chorus, she —
Some cabaret or revue
Direct from Gay Paree.
She straight unbuttoned her blouse,
And before she had scarce begun,
My uncle uttered that naughty word
That the sailor said to the nun.'

'In the war-crazy dollar-capitalist degenerate Western world there is a terrible housing shortage, so that many people have to live together in tiny tumbledown rooms for which they have to pay almost their whole salary. Consequently the little boy's uncle was obliged to have a very rude girl living with them, and he could not turn her out because if he did he would be thrown into prison. However, she was so rude that in the end the poor old uncle was driven to utter the ugly word that the dreadful nun had forced the good sailor to say.'

> 'And now I think it's time
> I told you the word at last.
> You've waited more than long enough,
> Although I've sung this fast.
> It's nothing very blue;
> No maiden cheek need blush;
> The censor would not notice it
> If he read this through in a rush.
> It's a simple four-letter word.
> You know it, every one:
> "Tush!" was the simple expletive
> That the sailor said to the nun.'

It took some time for Batjusjov to translate the last verse. He seemed rather confused when the children crowded round him, asking what it was that the sailor said to the nun. 'The sailor said: "Long live Stalin,"' he answered at last.

Pedersen asked if he should sing them another folk song, but the children showed no desire to hear more, and as Batjusjov was absolutely exhausted and looked very pale, they hurried on to the next brewery without visiting any more children's playrooms.

A few days later Count Frederick received a communication saying that Comrade Pedersen had been sent to a home for inebriates.

'From this we may learn,' said Engelsen, 'that when the

poor people from the capitalist world arrive in the Marxist paradise, they very soon collapse because they are unprepared for so much happiness.'

Count Frederick did not answer this, but he had to admit to himself that he did not feel quite normal and that he saw the tall, fair-haired Vera everywhere throughout the day. When the soft summer wind stroked his cheek while he crossed the Red Square, he thought it was the smooth skin of Vera's belly caressing him. When the vodka ran down his throat, he thought that it was Vera's tongue in search of new discoveries. When he laid his hands on the plush arm of one of the easy chairs in the Balaclava Hotel, he thought he was touching Vera's behind.

It soon became obvious that Vera had changed too. Her hair was no longer bundled into a tight bun at the nape of her neck, but fell down over her shoulders like apple blossom in windy weather. Count Frederick bought a frock from someone on the staff of the Danish Embassy, and managed to procure from various other embassies a pair of silk stockings, a pair of high-heeled shoes, and a summer coat. All the good Moscow citizens turned round and looked after her with tears in their eyes.

When Count Frederick and Vera walked across the Red Square he asked her to walk in front of him. The first time she obeyed because she did not know the reason — which was that in the tight skirt she now wore she wriggled her behind like a cropped puppy-dog, and it was impossible to say whether the sun was enjoying itself more on Vera's natural curves or on those of the golden balls and bulbous spires of St Basil's Cathedral. When Vera saw his expression she called him a degenerate Western beast and took his arm with great determination.

No one had seen Mr Phrederickh Phrederickhsen for several days, when one morning Count Frederick received a communication from the Ministry of State Security to the effect that they had been forced to send him to a hospital for nervous disorders because he continued to say that he

wished to see a collective farm and it had proved impossible to get him to say anything else.

Pellesen had not turned up since the incident with the vodka bottle on the first evening.

Ole Windbagsen, however, worked on persistently, jotting down a great many facts in his diary. He photographed the only all-marble station on the underground railway, and also the Red Square, the Kremlin, and Lenin's Tomb, and he visited all the large shops in the city. There were not many goods on display, nor were there many customers, and Windbagsen was therefore able to record the following truth about the Soviet Union: 'They do not make a great show of their goods, nor do they try to tempt people into buying what they do not need by wasting time on gaudy displays. Moreover, the inhabitants of Moscow are so well supplied that there is no need to queue, as in the Western countries, to get a bit of clothing on one's back.'

In one department of a big store, however, he was surprised to find a turbulent crowd and a queue stretching several hundred yards up and down the stairs. It turned out that a consignment of American nylons was on sale. In the crowd he saw several elderly ladies sitting on camp stools that they had brought with them and opening sandwiches. He wrote in his journal: 'The women of Moscow shop in a more dignified way than our own, but this does not mean that they are uninterested in novelties and foreign goods. Although they know perfectly well that no foreign products can compete with their own in quality, they show such a lively curiosity in the fashions and habits of other nations that they will wait patiently for several hours for a chance to study these goods.'

To document the Russian women's radiant patience and peace-loving interest in other nations, Windbagsen took a couple of pictures of the old women on camp stools. When he left the shop a little later he was arrested and taken to the headquarters of the secret police. A few days later Count Frederick was informed that Ole Windbagsen had been caught red-handed taking photographs for the benefit of a hostile power and that he was now in prison on a charge of espionage.

The Count tried to find Batjusjov to get more detailed information about the missing members of the delegation, but Batjusjov had also vanished without trace. No one knew anything about him, no one had even heard his name. When the Count mentioned this to Engelsen, Engelsen smiled in a superior fashion and said that Pernille too had vanished without trace.

'Why shouldn't she get a little fun out of this trip as well?' he demanded.

'That does not explain why neither the department dealing with delegations, nor the Ministry of the Interior, nor the Ministry for State Security, has ever heard of anyone called Batjusjov.'

'Might that not be because Soviet secretariats and ministries have a certain sympathy for affairs of the heart? They too are human, my boy, and apparently they are rather more human than our officials at home. In this country they take love into account.'

'If only they did,' sighed Count Frederick, and felt a shiver of erotic delight. 'As a matter of fact, I don't mind about Ole Windbagsen, do you?'

Engelsen thought for a while and then said: 'No, I couldn't bear him either. But I am sorry about Pedersen and Phrederickhsen. They were both good, cheerful, clever Danes. So was Pellesen, for that matter — he was absolutely trustworthy.'

'What shall we do?'

'Let us wait and see what happens. No doubt everything will sort itself out. And kiss Comrade Vera from me,' he added, looking round to find a subjectively pretty waitress.

Nothing sorted itself out, for nothing happened, and when one day Engelsen too disappeared, Count Frederick sought an interview with Commissar Jakovlevitch, who was said to be very influential in the secret police. He was a low-born, broad-shouldered man with thin hair and a choleric face. When the Count asked if he knew Batjusjov, he answered: 'Do you think I go about with two hundred and twenty thousand names in my head?'

'As far as I know, Batjusjov is an official and has certain connections with the police,' said the Count.

'Do you think I go round with the names of twenty thousand officials in my head? I have never even heard of anyone called Batjusjov.'

'We might perhaps postulate that there really is a Batjusjov,' suggested the Count.

'Certainly, if you insist on it, but don't you think that there are enough people in the world already?'

'More than enough, Mr Commissar, but I have a special interest in this hypothetical Batjusjov. He disappeared at about the same time as my good friends Engelsen and Miss Pernille, together with several other members of the delegation.'

'Engelsen came to the Soviet Union under false pretences,' said the commissar. 'He concealed the fact that he spoke Russian, and we have verified that he has carried on conversations with a number of suspected persons. He will be accused of espionage.'

'I did not think that there were any suspected persons in the Soviet Union,' said the Count, very much surprised.

'Perhaps you do not realize that there are foreign embassies here?'

'I have heard as much,' said the Count. 'But is it a punishable offence to speak Russian in Russia?'

'Is that a joke?'

'Yes, of course. That goes without saying,' answered the Count politely.

Jakovlevitch flushed, the strong red colour rising quickly from his throat to his cheeks, and so to his thinly-covered cranium, where it vibrated for a time and then subsided equally quickly beneath his coat collar.

'Engelsen should have stated on arrival that he spoke Russian,' he said sternly.

'He did, but the hypothetical Batjusjov said that Engelsen's Russian was a dialect he did not understand.'

'You are either very naive or very cunning,' said the commissar. 'As no Batjusjov has ever existed, your argument hardly holds water, does it?'

'It would seem that my naivety is most in evidence at the moment,' said the Count, 'but that will decrease with the years.'

'You want to suggest perhaps that Engelsen and the hypothetical Batjusjov were in league with each other?' asked the commissar intelligently.

'Only in so far as Engelsen showed great tolerance for the hypothetical Batjusjov's advances to Miss Pernille.'

'Aha! Madame Pernille is a very dangerous lady,' said the commissar, smacking his lips.

'In that way, yes.'

'What do you mean by that?' asked the commissar, becoming intelligent again.

'I fell for her myself once — many times, in fact. Her charms are very convincing. The hypothetical Batjusjov certainly allowed himself to be convinced, and so did one of my many delegates who has disappeared, Mr Pellesen.'

'Pellesen is a Stalinist agent-provocateur,' said the commissar.

'Will he be accused of espionage too?'

'Why else do you think he came to the Soviet Union? You are certainly right when you say you're naive.'

'He was invited.'

'You mean, he allowed himself to be invited. There is a difference.'

'Perhaps he also is naive?'

'Very naive.'

'I think you are right. Indeed, it is amazing how many naive people there are in the world.'

'And what do you mean by that?'

'I am thinking of all those who allow themselves to be invited to the Soviet Union.'

'That is not a joke.'

'It was not meant to be.'

The ugly red colour, like that of a well-boiled lobster, ran once or twice up and down Jakovlevitch's face.

'I do not wish to mix myself up in the internal quarrels of the communists,' continued the Count, 'but I should appreciate it very much if you would release Engelsen and Miss Pernille as soon as possible. The same applies to the other members of the delegation. The hypothetical Batjusjov may go on being hypothetical as far as I am concerned, but I should be glad if you would be kind enough to thank him for the excellent work he did for us. If it is any easier, you may make the thanks hypothetical as well.'

'You are very kind,' said the commissar, looking most embarrassed. 'Good afternoon.'

'Good afternoon, and many thanks for all your help,' answered the Count, bowing.

The commissar's mouth moved feebly and his face had a sudden attack of scarlet fever.

Late that evening Vera observed in a tired but unmistakably amorous voice that the varieties of Danish humour seemed infinite. 'But I do not think the secretariat is going to approve of the instruction you have given me,' she added. 'I should also prefer to keep all the variations to myself. I am no longer a good communist — it is frightful! And the alarm clock has stopped.'

The Count kissed the pole stars.

'We might marry,' said Vera, suddenly animated, 'and then you could take me back with you to humorous Denmark, couldn't you?'

The Count stopped kissing the pole stars and felt uncomfortable. He remembered clearly what his grandfather had said about falling in love but never marrying, and he realized that it was extremely sound advice.

'No,' he said, 'I cannot do that, for if I did I am afraid I might not stay in love with you.'

'Is that a joke?'

'It sounds like one, but it isn't.'

'You are a scoundrel.'

'Yes,' answered the Count, and kissed the giant poppy in the newly mown lawn of her face.

'I won't have anything more to do with you.'

'How well I understand you,' answered the Count, and kissed her swanlike neck.

'I really ought not to have anything more to do with you.'

'Of course not,' said the Count, and kissed the two nestlings.

'I ought not to do anything more than speak to you.'

To this the Count answered nothing at all. Instead he laid his cheek against her belly, and thought that it was the soft summer wind across the Red Square.

'You do not regret anything?' he asked.

'Of course not. Does it feel like that?'

'No,' he answered, 'it doesn't.'

'Nevertheless you are a liar,' she said. 'You see, I am not so lacking in humour as you think.'

'Then that makes you a liar also.'

'Your eyes were so blue,' she said.

Next morning they were both arrested. Vera Kovalof was accused of neglecting her duty in connection with her educational studies of Danish humour, and of having exceeded her authority with regard to the educational methods employed. She was given ten years' hard labour. Count Frederick was accused of having had degenerate, dollar-capitalist and debasing intercourse with a young, innocent communist maiden, and also of espionage, and was given twenty years' hard labour.

The only remaining member of the delegation, Professor Friede, was escorted to the plane by two members of the N.K.V.D., both armed with tommy-guns, who stayed at the entrance to the cabin until the plane was ready to take off. They then gave him a sealed letter which he had to swear to deliver to the editorial offices of the communist newspaper *Land and People* as soon as he arrived in Copenhagen. This he did, and the next day the following paragraph appeared:

A delegation consisting of a number of well-known Danes of independent political outlook has just returned from a very rewarding tour of the Soviet Union. The members of the delegation wish to state: 'We have had opportunities for unrestricted travel in the Soviet Union, and have been met everywhere with overwhelming friendliness and frankness. We have also been able to speak freely to everyone with whom we wished to speak. We confirm that the collective farms of the Soviet Union have a higher productivity rate than any other farms in the world; that Soviet beer is the healthiest and best-flavoured beer in the world; that Soviet women are the most beautiful in the world and dress simply, but delightfully; that the big Soviet shops are well stocked with all sorts of goods; that there are no queues anywhere, and no disagreement between communists, either in the Soviet Union or outside it; and that there is full security so that persons do not disappear without trace, as in the Western World.'

Signed:

PHREDERICKH PHREDERICKHSEN (*Civil Servant*)

PEDERSEN (*Brewery Worker*)

OLE WINDBAGSEN (*Editor and Writer*)

PELLESEN (*Member of the Communist Party*)

FRIEDE (*Professor*)

Professor Friede visited the offices of the newspaper the

next day and declared that he had neither seen nor signed the resolution in question.

The editor looked at him compassionately. 'My dear Professor, you must be very absent-minded. Have you forgotten that you came to this very office and handed the resolution to me in person?'

'I had no idea what was in the letter.'

The editor rang for an ambulance, and the attendants carried the shrieking and struggling professor out and took him to a mental hospital. It was found, however, that — apart from being exceedingly absent-minded — he was quite normal, so he was discharged. The professor then visited a large number of other newspapers. They were very charming to him, but they took no notice of what he said.

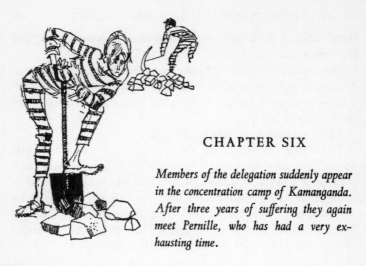

CHAPTER SIX

Members of the delegation suddenly appear in the concentration camp of Kamanganda. After three years of suffering they again meet Pernille, who has had a very exhausting time.

WHEN Count Frederick arrived at the concentration camp of Kamanganda in the north-east corner of Siberia, he met Engelsen, who had been given fifteen years' hard labour, Pellesen, who had been sentenced indefinitely, Ole Windbagsen, who had been given five years, and Pedersen, who had not been sentenced at all but had to be put somewhere.

'If only I had a beer,' sighed Pedersen. 'All those injections they gave me. Only God knows how thirsty I am. If only I had a beer.'

The Count met Phrederickh Phrederickhsen in the hutments reserved for the mentally deranged. Phrederickhsen grinned all over his face when the Count greeted him. 'I want to see a collective farm,' he said.

'Then look around you. This is a good enough example.'

'Many thanks,' answered Phrederickhsen, 'I am looking forward to seeing a collective farm.'

'Stop that nonsense, Phrederickhsen, and wake up!'

'Many thanks. I want to see a collective farm,' answered Phrederickhsen, and wandered off, smiling.

Batjusjov also was in the camp.

'Pernille,' he sighed, almost choking, when he saw Count

Frederick. 'Such breasts, what curves! She could easily have turned me into a Stalinist.'

'Where is she now?'

'Over there.' He pointed to some huts lying rather apart and surrounded with barbed wire. 'I see her now and again, and then I wail so loudly that they have to shut me up. Such breasts, such curves ... '

'Is she comfortable?'

'I don't know. But she still looks as if she were made of — of — '

'Melons?'

'Yes, yes, exactly. Melons. Last night the sirens had gone wrong, and they took me up into the watchtower and made her walk along below me, and I wailed so loudly that the whole camp heard me. Perhaps I shall get a job as siren wailer. Melons, yes of course.'

'Do you know anything about Vera Kovalof?' asked the Count.

'Don't think of her any more,' answered Batjusjov. 'She was given ten years' hard labour in a first-class brothel which has been specially set up for important visitors from the Chinese Republic. You must have given her a very good education. If I were you, I should bring forward that point when you apply for a reprieve after your first five years.'

Count Frederick sighed deeply, and tried to give up thinking of pole stars, swanlike necks, nestlings and soft summer winds over the Red Square.

To escape from these sweet memories, he looked up Ole Windbagsen and asked him what in the world he had done to get himself sent there.

'I simply cannot understand it,' answered the author.

'It is certainly very difficult to understand,' said Pellesen. 'The truth about the Soviet Union is not so simple.'

'And what about you, Engelsen?' asked the Count.

In the few weeks he had been in Kamanganda Engelsen had already become a great deal thinner. He was not enjoying himself. He was not cut out for tree-felling.

'Perhaps it was our own fault,' he answered. 'If we had acted differently, or if we had better understood the psychology of the Russians, we should probably not be here.'

'In the best of all possible worlds?'

'We must not judge, dear boy. What do we know of conditions outside this camp? Theoretically they may be like Paradise. There are prisons and criminals in every country.'

'Do you feel like a criminal?'

'Certainly not, but I am convinced that the whole thing is due to a misunderstanding. We shall soon get out. If only I were not so everlastingly hungry.'

For the next three years they worked fourteen hours out of the twenty-four, lived on cabbage soup, and suffered constantly from the fifty or more known forms of inflammation and diarrhoea. Ole Windbagsen became hysterical and was put in the division for the mentally deranged, together with Phrederickhsen. Pellesen had a good constitution, and was sufficiently stout-hearted to keep going. Pedersen suffered constantly from a disastrous thirst. For the first year Engelsen was like an old, outworn elephant, and his skin became loose enough to accommodate several others besides himself; but thanks to a highly developed sense of diplomacy, he managed to get posted to the kitchen, which was a good thing for all his friends. Pedersen was able to get more to drink, and Pellesen and Count Frederick got extra rations, which could be exchanged for shoes, clothes, and cigarettes. They survived.

Late in the summer of their third year the camp was visited by a group of Danish editors-in-chief, who had been invited to the Soviet Union so that they might see with their own eyes that it was not as bad as they said it was in their papers. For two months before the visit the working time in the camp was stepped up to sixteen hours out of the twenty-four. During those two extra hours the prisoners had to paint the huts, dig new latrines, clean out the infirmary, patch the prisoners' clothes, and build a platform where the prison orchestra, which had been hurriedly assembled, was to play to the guests.

Two days before the visit a number of lorries arrived with rolls of turf, boxes of plants, and white-painted garden seats, which were all set out charmingly around the huts, so that Pedersen felt as though he were back in the Garden Club to which he had belonged at home. Then the most unpresentable-looking prisoners, all the Danes, and the sick in the infirmary were taken away in the empty lorries to another camp, which then became still more overcrowded, thus raising the death-rate from the usual thirty per cent to about fifty per cent. The orchestra had its first rehearsal on the last evening, but two of the musicians, who had not seen a piece of music, much less played it, during the thirty-five years they had been in the camp, played a wrong note once or twice and were sent to hard labour in some coal mines near the Arctic Circle.

When the editors arrived, the remainder of the prisoners were marshalled into two long lines, so that the editors could march up and down and feel like generals at a parade, or perhaps like farmers at a cattle market. The Danish national anthem was played, and also the 'International', and all had tears in their eyes, or at least some of the editors had. Then the editors were given the opportunity to chat to some of the prisoners, who had arrived from the Ministry of State Security the previous day and had spent the night in the spring-cleaned infirmary to get acclimatized to the conditions. They all said that they were most comfortable and were grateful for the very mild sentences they had been given. There were no political prisoners among them, they said, only criminals. The prisoners told the editors about the various crafts they were learning, and added that they received the same wages as Soviet workers outside the camp. As proof, they produced some bank books which had been distributed by the camp's bank, and which all showed a fairly tidy credit balance.

After that one of the editors made a speech in which he

expressed his great admiration for the pioneer work of the Soviet prison authorities and promised to write fully about all that the Danes could learn from the Soviet Union. Finally, the editors enjoyed some refreshments in the camp canteen, which was usually the Commandant's dining-room, but had been cleared of its Renaissance furniture in honour of the day's events and furnished with garden seats hastily brought in from outside.

When the delegation was about to leave the camp, however, a minor incident took place. Ole Windbagsen, who was not always equally mad, had ferreted out what was happening in a lucid interval. As the prisoners in the mental division had not been removed because it was too troublesome and there was no need for them to be on view, he was still in the camp on this eventful day. He outwitted the guards and ran towards the editors in the square, shouting despairingly that he was Danish. He did not reach the group, however, for he was quickly recaptured. The Commandant explained that he was a mentally deranged student who had studied Danish but had suddenly gone crazy and murdered an old woman. Now he thought he was Danish, and had entirely forgotten his mother tongue.

'The strangest things can happen to people,' said one of the editors, shaking his head.

'Yes, indeed,' said all the others, and nodded energetically. Then they all entered the long black cars which so strikingly resembled Count Frederick's father's Packard, and drove away to see more Soviet wonders.

Batjusjov told his Danish friends all about this when they came back to Kamanganda.

Although Ole Windbagsen had not managed to make any impression on the Danish editors, the camp authorities became rather nervous of keeping Danish prisoners, and as they apparently had too good a constitution to be killed off in the usual way by means of starvation and tree-felling, it was decided to exchange them with some communists from Franco's concentration camps in Spain. They were therefore summoned before the Commandant and told to pack their belongings.

'What belongings?' asked Count Frederick, and was condemned to ten strokes of the knout.

'We should much prefer to be exchanged with Denmark,' said Pedersen.

'We have no exchange agreement with Denmark,' answered the Commandant.

'Perhaps you could make one?' suggested Pedersen, and was given ten strokes of the knout.

'How could they when there is no one to exchange with?' said Pellesen, and was given ten.

Engelsen said nothing, but when he saw that Ole Windbagsen did not mean to say anything either, he felt forced to speak. 'It has been a very interesting experience for us,' he said, and was given ten of the very best.

'I want to see a collective farm,' said Phrederickhsen, and was given a cuff on the side of the head.

Pernille was also thrown into the cattle truck that was to take them to Odessa, and when she heard the voices of her friends in the darkness, she stumbled around trying to find their cheeks to kiss.

'My goodness, Engelsen, what has happened to you?' she cried, horrified, when she found the remains of his face.

'I have been working, my girl,' said Engelsen. 'In the Soviet prison camps they take great trouble to see that prisoners have no time to regret their lost freedom. But as far as I can feel, you are in excellent condition.'

'Alas, yes,' answered Pernille, 'but I have had a very exhausting time. The Russians are a most exacting people and extraordinarily thorough. When I was arrested, the commissar who interrogated me said that he must examine me to find out whether I had hidden any arms or secret papers about my person. He examined me very energetically, and even pushed his finger into my mouth and loosened all my teeth in case I had a secret pivot-tooth where I could hide a micro-film. Then he raped me, and said that it was the surest method of assuring himself that I had nothing hidden there either. When he had finished his examination, he wanted me to sign some documents which said that I acknowledged that I had been spying for an enemy country. I refused, and he then sent me to another commissar, who was very stern and whose face went the colour of a pink corset when he saw me.'

'Was his name Jakovlevitch?' asked the Count.

'Yes,' said Pernille, 'and he was still more thorough. During the last and most exhausting part of the examination he showed me the document and told me to sign, but I still refused. Then he gave me ten strokes of the knout, and after that I signed because the knout was so very disagreeable.'

'Very disagreeable,' echoed Engelsen.

'Then I was condemned to ten years' hard labour and sent to Kamanganda, where the Commandant kept up the examination for three years running. In return, I was given plenty to eat, and had to wash once a month. I was given to understand that this was a tremendous privilege.'

'Tremendous,' said Engelsen.

'In the Soviet Union one learns to appreciate the simplest things, doesn't one, Engelsen?' said the Count.

'How bitter your voice has become, Count,' said Pernille. 'We have all aged quite a bit since we last met.'

Engelsen sighed deeply.

'My life for a beer,' said Pedersen.

After several weeks in the cattle truck, they reached Odessa, where they were all taken on board a Russian steamer. The Captain inspected the prisoners before they were stowed away in the hold, with the exception of Pernille who was to go to the Captain's cabin for examination.

During the journey to Spain Engelsen became very ill, but his friends could not see what he needed as there was no light in the hold. He ran a high temperature which they tried to bring down by applying cold compresses, made by dipping their clothes in the stinking bilge-water which ran over the floor of the hold. Engelsen was unconscious most of the time, but now and again he came to. Count Frederick sat beside him night and day to comfort and help him as best he could.

'We are scarcely likely to survive a stay with the fascists,' said Engelsen.

'They cannot be worse than the communists,' answered the Count consolingly.

'Theoretically there is a great difference. We must never forget that in theory the Marxists have created the best of all worlds.'

'Unfortunately Kamanganda was not particularly theoretical.'

'A long list of unfortunate misunderstandings led to our arrival in Kamanganda. Our sufferings there were a regrettable, but accidental, departure from theory. In Spain, on the other hand, the departure from this theory is the theory itself.'

'We are not likely to notice the distinction, my dear Engelsen.'

'None the less, we must keep it firmly in mind so that we do not become disillusioned. We must never give up hope of a better world,' said Engelsen, and relapsed into unconsciousness.

Pellesen was lucky enough to arouse the pity of one of the guards while they were in the Mediterranean, when the temperature in the lower hold rose to 113 degrees Fahrenheit. Between them, they arranged that one night, when the ship was close to the coast of Sicily, the guard would forget to bolt the door of the hold so that the prisoners could sneak up on deck and jump overboard.

Ole Windbagsen said he could not swim; there was no point in taking Phrederickhsen in his deranged state; Engelsen was too ill; and Count Frederick would not leave Engelsen. Besides, he did not wish to leave until he knew what had happened to Pernille. That left Pellesen and Pedersen, who slipped off one night when the guard had told them that they were only a few miles off the coast.

'A beer will be good when we meet again,' said Pedersen.

'There are a number of things that will be good,' said Pellesen.

'Do not judge too harshly, dear friends,' said Engelsen, 'and send us a couple of deep-frozen steaks and some sugared Bayonne hams. Perhaps you will be able to arrange through the Embassy to send a complete dinner to whichever concentration camp we end up in, and if so, I think I would prefer Veau à la Mode. Kindly write down the recipe, Pellesen, so that you do not forget. Take a pound of shoulder of veal and half a breast of veal cut into pieces and fried lightly in butter until it looks like a young girl's breasts at the beginning of the summer holidays. Then sprinkle a tablespoonful of flour over the meat and blend it in, add a generous portion of chopped onion and a little finely-chopped parsley, thin it down with good stock, add a bouquet garni, season with salt and pepper, and leave the whole thing to simmer for about an hour. When the sauce has begun to thicken, stir in a cupful of freshly prepared tomato purée and continue the cooking over a low fire until the sauce, which should be thin and smooth, has attained a suitable consistency, which means that it should feel as deliciously soft on the lips as Pernille's kisses — with which I believe you are only too well acquainted. Add a dozen small chipolatas and some pigs' trotters stuffed with truffles and baked in butter, together with a pound of mushrooms — although I can add those myself half an hour before we are going to eat it. And don't forget to send us some croûtons of French bread fried in butter. Can you remember that, Pellesen?'

'Certainly, Engelsen, certainly. Are there any other dishes you would like?'

'Entrecôte à la Esterhazy,' said Engelsen, 'but in that case you must tell the cook not to forget to cut the celery into julienne strips, because all too often the cook makes do with parsley roots. A little Homard à la Pot-bouille with poached fillets of sole in white wine would not be too bad either.'

'How about a bit of hash?'

'All right, all right, but not too often. And it would un-doubtedly help if you sent us some Oysters à la Belon first.'

'As you wish, Engelsen.'

'I will send you Sole Meunière, and a case of beer,' said Pedersen.

'Life is wonderful,' sighed Engelsen, and sank into a long, quiet sleep.

Pellesen and Pedersen succeeded in jumping overboard and swimming the distance to the coast of Sicily, where they were kindly received and quickly flown home to Copen-hagen. Those who have been communists or been accus-tomed to drinking a case of beer per day, and have then spent three years in Kamanganda, can exceed the normal human limits — especially when the rest of the party are en route for a concentration camp in Spain.

CHAPTER SEVEN

Count Frederick and his companions spend a year in the concentration camp of Alcazar and thus have an opportunity of comparing the various forms of slave labour current in the modern world. The Count is lucky as a bullfighter.

WHEN the Russian steamer anchored at a Spanish port, the prisoners were brought up on deck. The Captain counted them four times, checked their number with his papers, and finally concluded that there must be a mistake somewhere in the counting.

'The other two drowned in the bilge-water,' Count Frederick offered.

'Bring up the corpses,' commanded the Captain, 'I must have a receipt for them from the Spaniards.'

'I'm afraid the rats have eaten them.'

'That's too bad,' said the Captain irritably. 'It's always the same when I take on prisoners. Will you sign here for the two persons used as rat-fodder?'

'Where is Miss Pernille?' asked the Count.

'Oh, she died too,' answered the Captain, 'but you needn't worry about her: I've got a receipt for her. I sold her corpse to a Libyan embalmer who wanted something to practise on.'

When Engelsen heard this he lost consciousness again, for he loved Pernille dearly. Later on the Count reminded him comfortingly that as the receipts for Pellesen and Pedersen were false, there was good reason to suppose that Pernille's was too, and that she was alive in Libya and in the best of health.

Before the prisoners were handed over to Franco's secret police, the Captain gave them a lecture on dialectical materialism.

'What do you think of this steamer?' he asked when he had finished his lecture.

'It is a rusty old coffin-ship,' answered the Count.

'Then either you have not understood a word of what I have been saying,' answered the Captain, 'or you are an obstinate, lying capitalist. If you say that this is a rusty old coffin-ship, you have isolated a purely temporal factor from its true context and been guilty of a metaphysical judgment; if you say that this is a super-modern, well-kept and most efficient steamer, you are wrong as far as the temporal aspect is concerned, for it is not at the moment modern, well-kept or efficient, but you are right dialectically because it very soon will be. Soviet people live in the future, and in the future this steamer will be a model of modern ship-building technique. Will you now explain to me how you would give a dialectically true description of your sojourn in the Soviet Union?'

The Count, who was not only polite but exceedingly intelligent, answered:

'If I say that we have been in a frightful, inhuman, lousy concentration camp where we were starved and ill-treated, I should be lying dialectically, even though it is true in actual fact. If, on the other hand, I say that we found ourselves in a modern educational camp, where we received instruction on a purely voluntary basis and worked towards a better understanding of dialectical materialism and the greatness of the Soviet Union, I should be speaking the truth, for although such a camp does not yet exist, it may be the only form of punishment that the Soviet Union will recognize and use in the future. To recognize the future in the present is true dialectic, and therefore the real truth.'

'Excellent,' answered the Captain. 'I am delighted to have driven all traces of capitalist mendacity out of you. You will now be well armed against every fascist temptation.'

Ole Windbagsen said that he could not understand any of it.

Phrederickhsen said that he wanted to see a collective farm.

Engelsen said nothing, for he had not yet recovered from his grief at the loss of Pernille.

However, the Captain comforted the Count by telling him that he was sure he would later have plenty of opportunity for instructing his friends in the blessings of dialectical materialism.

The prisoners were handed over to the Spaniards, who gave the Captain a group of communists in return. The communists were stuffed into the lowest hold for transport and subsequent treatment in Kamanganda or other similar places.

'In the best of all possible worlds there would appear to be a constant cultural exchange between friendly nations,' said the Count.

Engelsen did not seem to have heard this, so he naturally made no reply.

With a suitable number of kicks and blows the fascist guards chivvied the four Danes into a cattle truck standing ready on a siding in Barcelona station. There were already about fifty prisoners of various nationalities in the dark, stinking interior, so that they were all obliged to climb over one another, but as those who were already there seemed to take this lying down, the Count inferred that most of them were dead already. It was unbearably hot in the truck, and during the two days that it was left standing in the siding the prisoners were given nothing to eat or drink, which caused Ole Windbagsen to howl and Count Frederick to suggest that they might each try to lick their own sweat to lessen their thirst.

'I'm afraid my taste organs are too sensitive to do any such thing,' answered Engelsen.

'Your senses seem to be extremely undemocratic for the times we live in,' said the Count.

'There you are wrong. My taste organs are adjusted at that level which the Marxist-socialist community will attain some day in the future, where no one will be forced to eat anything except the most delicious dishes. That I have fallen into fascist hands at the moment and am therefore obliged to prostitute my senses, only goes to show that all societies other than the Marxist are imperfect and degraded.'

'Yes, of course,' said the Count, nodding. 'I ought to have said that myself now that I have been so well instructed in dialectical materialism. But how do you explain the far from perfect taste of the cabbage soup in Kamanganda?'

'You disappoint me,' answered Engelsen. 'In every community there are bad men; admittedly there is a smaller proportion in the socialist countries than in all the others — but even so there are still some. To re-educate these people, it is necessary that they should be made to notice for a time an unpleasant difference between life outside the rehabilitation camps and life inside them. As the food we were given in the Soviet Union was perfectly delicious, the food in Kamanganda was naturally less good for purely educational reasons.'

'I admit I should be positively glad of even Kamanganda cabbage soup at this moment.'

'There you are,' answered Engelsen. 'We shall soon be longing to be back in Siberia.'

'In Siberia we longed to be back in Denmark,' said the Count. 'But perhaps the moral of all our sufferings is that we should learn that longing is the most important of human needs. My grandfather, Count Hector, said something of the sort in his time.'

'That is a capitalist way of thinking that you must give up as soon as possible,' said Engelsen, disturbed. 'Longing is a purely temporary phenomenon which can be utilized to bring about more quickly the perfect, equal, and collective society; it will disappear the moment our political aims have been realized.'

'Batjusjov's and Vera Kovalof's longings would seem to invalidate that statement.'

'Nonsense!' said Engelsen angrily. 'I may remind you that they were both arrested, which means that they were not sound Soviet citizens.'

'Vera Kovalof was exceptionally sound.'

'She had a depraved mind.'

'Then I am afraid I set great store by a depraved mind.'

'This discussion is both rude and personal,' said Engelsen. 'We must try to avoid such vulgarities. It must be our fascist surroundings that are corrupting us.'

'This place certainly stinks of corruption,' answered the Count.

On the third day the door was opened so that the dead prisoners could be taken out, which left the survivors so much more room that they had no need to sit on top of one another.

'The death-rate in the fascist cattle trucks seems to be somewhat higher than in the communist ones,' the Count observed.

'Naturally,' answered Engelsen.

The prisoners were each given a tin bowl containing something that the Spanish guards claimed was potato soup.

'Apart from the difference in the theoretical claims regarding the basic substances of these soups, there is an amazing similarity between the communist and fascist love of liquid food,' said the Count.

'There have never been any potatoes in this rotten liquid,' answered Engelsen. 'On the other hand I often found pieces of cabbage in the Kamanganda soup.'

'Engelsen, you are nothing if not willing.'

After they had enjoyed the theoretically potato soup, their cattle trucks were coupled to a train and they began the journey up to the concentration camp of Alcazar on the high plateau of Castile. It took about as long as the journey from Siberia to Odessa, and the heat in the van increased appallingly as they worked their way across the dry, burning plain. Strangely enough, Engelsen seemed to become better every day, and although the long journey cost him at least twenty pounds of his Kamanganda fat, he was so cheered by the inefficiency of the fascist transport and prison system that his hunger seemed to trouble him less and less.

In Alcazar the Count and Engelsen were set to work at stone-breaking for fourteen hours a day, which caused Engelsen to say that he preferred felling trees.

'Surely the real point is that the working time is the same,' answered Count Frederick.

'The cubic weight of stone is greater than the cubic weight of fuel,' Engelsen replied.

The camp authorities soon discovered that Ole Windbagsen and Phrederickhsen were both quite unsuitable for any form of work, and they therefore took them to the division for the mentally deranged. Engelsen, on the other hand, who had a special flair for languages, soon learnt Spanish, and with the help of this and a little diplomacy he was fortunate enough to be given a job in the kitchen. This was a great advantage for him and the Count, because it meant that they could obtain double rations and exchange some of them for shoes, clothes, and tobacco. So again they survived.

After some months the camp authorities arranged a bullfight to amuse the guards and the prisoners. Those prisoners who had the courage and the desire to try their luck as matadors were promised in return that they would be released — if they survived.

For two months before the bullfight was to take place the working time was stepped up to sixteen hours out of the twenty-four. The extra hours were used for breaking stones to be used to build an amphitheatre down in the quarry.

The Count reported to the Commandant's office, and suggested that he should fight the biggest bull in return for freedom for himself and Engelsen if he succeeded in killing the animal.

When the Commandant heard that the Count knew nothing whatever about this sport, he agreed, and said that the Count, even though not a Spaniard, undoubtedly had a certain *grandezza*.

When Engelsen heard of the Count's decision, he was

very much upset and begged him anxiously to give up the crazy idea.

'Would you rather spend the rest of your days here?' asked the Count.

'There is always a third way out,' said Engelsen, 'and probably a less bloody one.'

'That is just what I am afraid there is not. I become daily more convinced that the evil in this world is singularly inescapable.'

'Not to hope is the greatest evil of all,' said Engelsen.

'Good,' answered the Count. 'Then let us set our brains to work and find a quick way out — in the arena.'

The day the bullfight took place Engelsen and the Count sat in the front row and carefully followed the many different ways in which the bull slit the bellies of the unfortunate matadors and the old, half-blind horses.

Engelsen was very nervous, but the Count smiled at him and reminded him that as their plan had been thought out by so dialectically well-trained a brain as Engelsen's own, it could not possibly go wrong.

'Dialectic is a philosophical method which is not designed to deal with bullfights,' answered Engelsen.

'When it can be used to turn unseaworthy coffin-ships into super liners, rotten water into nourishing cabbage soup, and Siberian concentration camps into institutes resembling universities, surely it can kill a dirty bull,' said the Count, and nodded encouragement to his tutor, who was holding his handkerchief up to his nose to avoid the dreadful stench that rose from the bloody arena.

'You are just like your grandfather,' said Engelsen. 'No wonder it takes a long time to improve the world.'

At long last they reached the highlight of the day: Count Frederick's fight with the largest and maddest of the bulls. The importance of this fight was emphasized by spreading fresh sand over the blood and dragging away the corpses of the slaughtered horses. Count Frederick was handed a rapier and he walked calmly out into the middle of the arena, his blue blood instinctively causing him to carry himself like a true Spaniard. The Commandant patted his stomach contentedly, and whispered to his wife that he had always thought that Danes were a type of dog which excelled at snapping at the legs of intruders, but that there were evidently human beings called Danes as well and they were perhaps not insignificant, even though they were not Spaniards.

The bull was let out into the arena and stood for some time gazing around rather confusedly, pawing the sand and staring hostilely at the Count, who went on standing there, straight and indifferent, returning the bull's gaze with a polite vigilance. Discontented murmurs were heard from the spectators, and at a sign from the Commandant some of the prisoners set to and goaded the bull from behind, while waving red rags in front of it. That helped. The bull roared, capered about in the arena, and concentrated his hostility on the Count.

Count Frederick moved round calmly so that he kept the bull in view. He held his left hand raised in the air, so that it looked as if he were walking on a tightrope, and this gave him an appearance of great elegance. The Spaniards were pleased by his attitude, and clapped. The bull took a deep breath and set off at a gallop towards the Count, but stopped halfway, turned as if it had something in its eye, tried again to stare at the Count, and finally gave it up. It seemed as if a sort of power radiated from him which stopped the bull and particularly affected its eyes. The Count advanced slowly towards the beast, while continuing to play with his left hand lifted high in the air. The bull turned and tossed its head to escape the sight of this hand, backed slowly until its rump knocked into the stone barrera, and began to roar in a heart-breaking manner.

All stared as if bewitched at this strange drama, and the Commandant's wife whispered to her husband that they really must spend their next summer holidays in Denmark. The bull now edged round the stone barrera, turning its head as if it were being slapped in the face, while the Count followed it soberly. To put an end to this game, he increased his speed, but the bull did the same, and soon the Count had to run as fast as he could to keep up with the beast. The spectators were doubled up with laughter and mocked the bull, who seemed aware of it.

The Count realized that things could not go on like this if he wished to keep up the good impression he had made. He therefore moved out again into the middle of the arena. There he knelt down and laid the rapier in front of him on the sand, putting both hands into his pockets. At this Engelsen started, for this meant that the Count could not use the plan he had worked out for him, which so far had succeeded beyond all expectations. The bull took courage and looked cautiously at the Count, and as it no longer felt hampered by any radiation, it moved nearer. Still nothing happened, and it was obvious that the bull had regained much of its unsympathetic character, roaring as if it had never been anything but an unconquerable, courageous bull, afraid of nothing. It snorted, and then set off at a wild gallop towards the Count, who rose but left the rapier lying on the ground. When the bull was a few yards from him, he again lifted his godlike left hand, which made the bull turn its head angrily so that it rushed past the Count, who wheeled round with an elegant gesture and watched its crestfallen rump delightedly.

'Olé!' shouted the spectators, and clapped.

The Commandant's wife turned round and whispered to her maid to arrange for this Dane to visit her the next time the Commandant went to Madrid on business.

'He's left his rapier behind,' someone shouted.

'He can hypnotize the animal,' shouted someone else.

'He is wonderful,' said the wives of the guards.

'He is a Count,' said the Commandant, 'and his family probably came from Spain.'

The Count's behaviour had created the right atmosphere, and those prisoners who had been chosen as assistants and

picadors but who had not so far displayed much enthusiasm
for their jobs, now ran out into the arena and danced round
the bull, waving their red capes. The bull shook its head,
pulled itself together, and set off after one of the men with
a red cape. The man was not quick enough, fell, became
entangled in his cape, and was lifted up on the bull's horns
and flung over the stone barrera. The spectators stamped
with fury and threw rotten tomatoes at the unfortunate man.

The bull looked round quickly for another victim and
picked out a picador, on an old, stiff-legged hack, who,
thanks to a pair of blinkers, could not see what was happening. The picador, who was a civil war veteran and had
therefore spent twenty years increasing his strength by

stone-breaking, held his lance firmly directed towards the knotted muscles in the animal's shoulder. The bull lowered its head and rushed forward, meaning to give the horse a good thrust in the stomach, but the picador's lance forced itself in, and the veteran leaned on the lance with all his strength and with the other hand lifted the kicking old hack into the air, swinging it out to one side so that the bull rushed in underneath without striking it. When the horse came down to earth again, it was so frightened that it farted violently and noisily right in Engelsen's face, so that his handkerchief was blown out of his fingers. Finding himself suddenly unprotected and surrounded by a very offensive smell, Engelsen remarked to his neighbour that he preferred the stink of Kamanganda's latrines.

'That was splendid,' answered his neighbour.

'What — the smell?' asked Engelsen, surprised.

The neighbour looked at Engelsen uncomfortably, and hastened to move his seat to another row.

'That was a fine suerte,' the spectators shouted, and clapped.

When the bull saw itself deprived of its horse-stomach, it looked round for compensation. Not far away was a white horse in the act of delivering some dry dung. The picador tried to interrupt this pleasant occupation, but the horse was much too occupied to react, and the bull steered unfalteringly and without being troubled by any distracting lances, straight into the belly of the horse, where it began to rootle round to some purpose. The picador tried to slip down to the other side of the horse to save his own belly from a similar fate, but he need not have worried, for the bull was far too busy to notice him. None of the other assistants or picadors seemed anxious to rescue the wretched horse, so the Count rushed forward and gave the bull a good whack on the rump with his rapier, which certainly did not please the beast. It pulled its horns out of the horse's guts and rushed at the Count, who promptly raised his left hand. This infuriated the bull; it jumped, and ran, and tried to rub its eyes with its forelegs, but to no avail. Maddened by a pain entirely incomprehensible to the spectators, it rushed at the Count, who wheeled elegantly round the animal's butting head while giving it one more stinging, satisfying blow with the rapier.

The enthusiasm in the arena ran high.

'What a Belmonte-like recorte,' shrieked the spectators. 'And without a cape! He is absolutely divine.'

The men banged one another on the back, and threw their tattered shoes high up in the air. It was the only form of clothing they could spare for the moment. The women became starry-eyed and their bodies grew damp.

When the other picadors saw what had happened to their companion, who was limping out of the arena after having his leg crushed beneath the dying horse, they removed themselves to a reasonable distance from the bull.

Then a trumpet sounded, which was a sign that the banderillero was about to appear. A man carrying two thin sticks on which were fixed bits of red paper fluttering in the wind moved forward towards the bleeding bull, who stared at him angrily. Then the animal lifted its tail and charged. The man stood leaning backwards with lifted arms, the sticks pointing vertically downwards towards the animal's bleeding shoulder; he might easily have been demonstrating to housewives how to carve a joint of beef. The bull rushed straight at him, but the man bent forward and thrust the sticks into the wound, so that Engelsen felt as if he were sitting in the dentist's chair and the drill had touched a nerve. Obviously the bull felt the same, for it tossed its head wildly and leaped up from the ground like a frog that has caught sight of a stork. The man raised himself on the sticks, which were now firmly planted in the animal's flesh, stretched out his arms, and swung out to the side while the bull ran past him.

The spectators jumped up on their stone seats, and shouted and yelled with excitement. The Commandant's wife whispered to her maid that she must remember to find out the name of the man with the sticks. But the Count was not forgotten, and soon there were shouts of 'Federico! Federico!'

Again Count Frederick moved out into the middle of the arena and was greeted with delighted shouts. The end was now in sight. While the banderillero had been doing his work, the Count had been watching the Commandant's wife with whom he had exchanged some of those glances that are international and not open to misinterpretation. He felt intensely sorry for the bull, and he had not the least desire to finish it off, but for the sake of the Commandant's wife's hospitable eyes and the freedom which had been promised to him and Engelsen, he decided to complete the murder in suitable style. He bowed deeply towards the Commandant's wife, and said:

'I dedicate this bull to you, Señor Commandante' (adding in Danish, 'You fat slave-dealer'), 'and to you, Señora' (adding, 'You lecherous little bitch'), 'and to the Spanish people, the most noble people in the world' (adding again in Danish, 'Which is possibly true, apart from their leaders').

All felt much honoured, though some wondered why it was that Engelsen laughed so violently.

The bull glared reluctantly at the Count, for its memories of him were not pleasant. It shut its eyes and reflected for a moment, flicked away the flies with its tail, cautiously opened its eyes again, and tried to follow the Count's movements by looking out of the corner of its eye. The blood poured down over its shoulders and forelegs, which seemed so unsteady, that it could easily have been thought drunk. The Count wished heartily that he were. The arena was very silent. The men leaned forward with their hands on their thin knees: the women twisted their fingers and sat, their mouths open, looking very stupid. The bull also opened its mouth, but instead of looking stupid, it merely looked more ferocious. It licked the froth from its muzzle with a long tongue. The Count would have liked to pat it and bandage it up, but he imagined to himself that the bull was Franco in disguise and that helped him to feel unsympathetic. Moreover, there was a certain resemblance between the face of the bull and the face of the Commandant, and that also made the sickening scene more tolerable. He swung the rapier round once or twice so that the sun glinted on it, making the bull start and move away from him, while at the same time it gave up glaring at him.

It is afraid of him, thought the Commandant's wife, and felt a sweet shiver run down her own backbone.

No more of this, said the Count to himself, or I shall never get hold of him, and he hid the rapier behind his back, advancing towards the bull with his left hand at the ready, that strange left hand that seemed to possess supernatural powers but which in reality only concealed a little bit of sound Danish shrewdness. When the bull saw that the rapier was no longer there, and that no unpleasant radiation came from the left hand, it pulled itself together and turned towards the Count, who quickly approached it. A few yards off he stopped and shouted 'Hi!' The bull answered by smacking its lips once or twice, and shaking its head.

'I am sick of all this,' the Count said to the bull, 'but if I do not do it, someone else will, and besides, enough bellies have been slit open for today.'

The bull nodded agreement.

'So let us get it over quickly without too much tom-foolery,' said the Count. 'It's about time that you and I and Engelsen all got away from this concentration camp.'

The bull nodded eagerly.

'You are so sensible that one might even put you down as being of Danish descent,' said the Count.

The bull shook its head.

Danish or Spanish, thought the Count, I can only hope that Engelsen was given the right information in the kitchen on how to kill you, my dear Ferdinand. 'Corto y derecho,' he told me, and plunge the rapier right down into the hollow between the bull's shoulder blades. 'It is no larger than a buttonhole,' he said. Worse luck!

'That campagnero must weigh at least a ton,' said a specta-
tor sitting behind Engelsen who knew nothing about bulls.

Engelsen sweated with apprehension, and thought that
however one looked at it, the bull weighed far too much,
except from the point of view of beef.

The bull had now decided to act. It lifted its tail, stamped
once or twice, arched its neck and charged. Count Frederick
managed to lift his left hand in time, which again made the
bull miss him and rush past. Unfortunately it went so
quickly that the Count had no time to drive the rapier home.

The enthusiasm of the crowd was now unbounded. 'What
a natural pase!' they shouted.

Engelsen thought that the Count had gone crazy and that
all this was highly unnatural.

'Now he's making a pase de pecho,' shouted the crowd.
'Look, look!'

The bull turned and again rushed madly at the Count,
who this time concentrated entirely on trying to find the
confounded spot between the shoulder blades where he
must strike. He did not even notice that the bull rushed
past him and that the bloody sticks grazed his chest; neither
did he discover where the rapier should go in.

'It is the finest pase de pecho we have ever seen,' shrieked the
crowd.

'It is absolutely absurd,' said Engelsen, but no one heard
him.

'He's much too close,' whispered the Commandant's wife
to her maid.

'He is a great matador,' said the Commandant.

I am a great bungler, thought the Count. If I don't find
that spot soon, we're done for.

The bull now stood with its legs wide apart and planted
heavily in the sand. It stared at the Count and glanced side-
ways at the uplifted left hand. Neither could make out what
the other was doing. It was indeed a difficult situation.
Neither of them was interested in fascists, much less in killing
or being killed, but a cruel fate forced them to appear before

their keepers to do just that. The Count told himself that this was not the moment to indulge in generalizations about existence, but rather to follow his grandfather's good advice to act according to one's natural instincts; in this case his natural instincts were all for survival, which meant that the bull must die. Somehow or other he must place himself where he would have time to locate the position of the hollow between the shoulder blades. If he could get the bull to circle round him for a few seconds, then there might perhaps be time enough.

He therefore ran over to one of the assistants and borrowed a red cape which he tied round his left arm. The bull gazed at him with interest. It held its head low, but happily not so low that the Count could not fix it with his eye. The bull did not stir. Only its eyes moved. It is as heavy and immovable as a Spanish locomotive, thought the Count as he approached with the red cape, which he still kept tied round his arm. Not until he was quite close to the bull did he unwind it and wave it about. The bull emerged from its trance and rushed at the cape, which the Count swung round in a circular movement. The bull followed at breakneck speed and made such a rapid hairpin bend around the Count that its legs almost shot from under it. The blood from its shoulder spattered the Count's prison uniform. The women shrieked, for they had all seen how blue the Count's eyes were. The men bellowed. The Commandant's wife grew very pale and sighed.

'He's as brave — as brave — as a Spanish Commandant,' said the Commandant.

While the bull whirligigged round Count Frederick the latter thrust the rapier down between its shoulder blades, but unfortunately it struck against the bone and shot out of his hand, falling to the ground some way off. The bull wheeled like lightning, but the magical left hand restrained it and the Count was able to recover his rapier in peace.

So it won't work, said the Count to himself. I shall have to think of something more drastic.

He followed the bull, waving the red cape. The bull gathered speed, and just as it ran at the red cape the Count caught it by the horns as it passed and swung himself on to the animal's back. The arena was almost beside itself with enthusiasm. Never had anything of the kind been seen before. The bull stopped and looked round in confusion. Where the devil was he now? It blinked once or twice to clear its sight, but no! Vanished, completely vanished.

These few seconds of astonishment cost the bull its life, for Count Frederick, who continued to sit astride the bull, thus had time to find the hollow between its shoulder blades and plunge the rapier in up to the hilt. His fingers went in with it, and when he drew the rapier out his hand was covered with blood. He felt the bull totter beneath him, jumped off, and saw it fall over, then lie still with its four legs straight up in the air. Immediately the prisoners, the guards and the guards' wives poured into the arena. The whole place was in an uproar. They rushed up to Count Frederick, chaired him and carried him round and round, shouting 'Federico, Federico!'

Engelsen dried the sweat from his brow and breathed freely at last. The Commandant's wife smiled sweetly to herself behind a big bunch of flowers that hid her face right up to the eyes, which certainly made no secret of their intentions. The bull's long tongue hung out of its bloody, foam-flecked mouth. There was a sickening smell. Count Frederick was carried out of the quarry. Everybody shouted and yelled and clapped. It was the only holiday of the year, and one or two of the prisoners actually discovered potatoes in their soup. It was a festival day in the concentration camp of Alcazar.

When all the spectators had at long last shrieked themselves hoarse and it was time to sleep, Count Frederick put his hand in his left pocket and pulled out the magnifying-glass that Engelsen had exchanged for a pail of potatoes. They decided to hide it carefully. One never knew when it might be useful.

CHAPTER EIGHT

Count Frederick waits on the Commandant's wife who instructs him as to Purgatory. A diplomatic swindle takes the Count and Engelsen off to Morocco.

After the lucky bullfight Count Frederick reminded the Commandant of his promise, but the Commandant said he must first go to Madrid to discuss their release with the Ministry for State Security. The Count expressed the hope that the Commandant would soon find reason to go to Madrid.

His hope was quickly fulfilled, but Engelsen warned him against the Commandant's wife, Doña Isabel.

'Vera Kovalof got you three years in Kamanganda,' he said.

'I should have ended up there anyhow,' answered the Count, 'and if I had not seduced Vera I shouldn't have a single pleasurable memory of my whole sojourn in the Soviet Union.'

'That is a very short-sighted view,' answered Engelsen. 'One should plan for one's whole life.'

'That would be very boring.'

'It is more important to be secure.'

'I think it is more important not to be bored,' said the Count, 'and for that reason I am now going to visit Doña Isabel, which I expect will be anything but boring. Besides, surely you agree with me that the cuckolding of our fascist Commandant is an attractive by-product?'

Engelsen was obliged to admit that this put a different complexion on the matter, but he added: 'Your view of existence is capitalist and superficial. Apart from the few privileged people, the world longs for security.'

'There is much to indicate that you are right,' answered

the Count, 'since both the Soviet Union and Spain have their Ministries of State Security. Nevertheless, I have been excessively bored in the two establishments run by these Ministries which I have had the opportunity to visit, and without feeling particularly secure in either of them.'

'There are various forms of security,' answered Engelsen. 'One must distinguish between them.'

'No doubt,' answered the Count, and hurried off to visit the Commandant's wife.

Doña Isabel received him well and looked lovely. Her eyes were like horizontal keyholes, black, compelling, narrow, and long, and when one gazed into them, one's own eyes watered just as if they had been exposed to a violent draught. Her wrists and ankles were small, supple and white, like birch branches, and her waist was so slender that it was possible to see both sides of a claret glass placed exactly behind her back.

'You are the loveliest woman I have ever seen,' said the Count.

'You undoubtedly say that to all women, so it can hardly be true,' she answered.

The Count thought that, judging by his Soviet experiences, this was only a truth, not a particular truth. On the other hand it might well be called a dialectic truth. Aloud he said:

'Your eyes are two secrets that a man must unceasingly seek to guess. The charm of your hands flashes like the silver keys of Heaven. Your feet are delicate and timid like the ears of a doe.'

'Oh,' she said, 'not only do you kill bulls like a Spaniard, but you also talk like one. Denmark must be very Spanish. Perhaps it is one of our former colonies?'

'Not noticeably,' answered the Count, 'but we prize Spanish women very highly.'

'Oh,' she said, 'but the Danes are not Catholics, are they? That is very sinful ... What you are trying to do now is also very sinful.'

'We are very fond of being sinful,' said the Count.

'Ah,' she said.

A little later she added: 'That will cost you seven years in Purgatory.'

'That's all right,' answered the Count. 'It can scarcely be worse than the four years I have spent in Kamanganda and Alcazar. How much do I get for this?'

'Ah!' she said.

And a little later: 'That will cost you fourteen years.'

'That makes twenty-one altogether,' said the Count.

'You are either a very courageous man or a very frivolous one.'

'A bit of both is probably nearest the truth.'

'If you go on as you have begun, you will probably burn in Purgatory for at least one hundred years,' said Doña Isabel, and blushed.

The Count stopped sinning for a moment and weighed up the cost.

'Isn't it possible to pay off some of the debt during one's lifetime?' he asked.

Doña Isabel nodded eagerly: 'For every Our Father that you say you will get let off a year's torments.'

'What a practical religion,' said the Count. 'My grandfather would have approved of it highly. Can I buy this indulgence beforehand?'

Doña Isabel's eyes narrowed so that one could almost hear her dark glance whistling through them.

'Certainly,' she whispered. 'How many are you going to say?'

'Two hundred down and the rest on account.'

'Oh,' groaned Doña Isabel, near to exhaustion. 'You must be contemplating an alarmingly great sin, mi Conde.'

'I certainly am,' confirmed Count Frederick, and began to pray.

When the Commandant arrived in Madrid, there was a great deal of fuss about the Danish prisoners in Alcazar.

Several applications had been received from the Danish Government on account of Pellesen's and Pedersen's insistent statements that five Danes were being held in Spanish prisons. At the moment it was most undesirable to quarrel with foreign countries because there was a war in progress with Morocco, and the Scandinavian countries were distinctly unsympathetic. Consequently, there was a certain amount of unease, and the situation was hardly improved when the Commandant of Alcazar stated that he had promised Count Frederick and Engelsen their freedom.

After a good deal of discussion, it was decided to answer that though they did inadvertently have two Danish prison-soners in their possession, Phrederickh Phrederickhsen and Ole Windbagsen, nothing was known of the other three. It was felt that these two could be freed without any particular risk, as they were both more or less insane, and also, since they had both been confined in the division for the mentally deranged, they could not say very much about the conditions in Spanish concentration camps in general. The Commandant, who was a true Spaniard, was not at all pleased with this decision. He had given his word to the Count, and the Count had shown himself to be a genuine nobleman.

At last the following solution was proposed. The war with Morocco meant that there were various Spanish soldiers being held by the Moroccans as prisoners of war, and if the two Danes were exchanged for two Spanish soldiers, the lives of two heroic Spaniards would be saved, and — at any rate formally — the promise kept to Count Frederick that he should be allowed to leave Alcazar. The Commandant was not at all pleased with this solution either, as it seemed to him unworthy of Count Frederick. He therefore decided to poison the Count and Engelsen before the exchange took place, to save them from any more undignified experiences. Then he went back to his faithful wife Doña Isabel and told her everything, with the result that the Count and Engelsen in future kept solely to their theoretically potato soup and did not enjoy any of the Red Cross parcels which unknown well-wishers suddenly sent them.

'You must own, Engelsen, that the type of security that Doña Isabel represents is not entirely senseless,' said the Count.

'In a fascist society everything is senseless,' answered Engelsen.

'I agree with you, but the same consideration seems to apply to all other societies.'

'My boy,' sighed Engelsen, 'you are heading for perdition.'

A few months later they were pushed into a cattle truck and taken to Algeciras, and from there they sailed to Tangier, and were then again locked into a cattle truck which took them to a prison camp near Marrakesh.

'We shall now be able to compare, not only Asiatic and European, but also African concentration camps,' said Count Frederick. 'We are certainly getting a very thorough knowledge of the penal systems of the modern world.'

CHAPTER NINE

Count Frederick and Engelsen work in a caravanserai. Engelsen makes himself popular with the camels, and unpopular with the Moroccans. They become a commodity with a rapid turn-over and end up in Saudi-Arabia.

THE Commandant of the Moroccan prison camp pushed the two newcomers into a dark dungeon for a few weeks, only relieved by half-an-hour's beating-up at five o'clock every morning. Several thousand years of Arabic culture had taught him that this treatment was the maximum that could be meted out to a human being without killing him, while at the same time it was not so bad as to unfit him for slave labour a few days later.

The Commandant, a practical and money-happy gentleman, afterwards hired out the prisoners to Moroccans against a small payment which found its way into his roomy pocket. The prisoners were not paid for their work, and were obliged to beg for their food or obtain it in some other way. If they were unable to do so and died from starvation, no one regretted it, for such a prisoner was not worthy of being an Arab's slave.

Count Frederick and Engelsen were hired out to a caravanserai, where they were put to tend the camels belonging to the caravans that arrived.

'The camel is a very human animal,' said Count Frederick, after he had associated for some time with the inhabitants of the caravanserai. 'It looks arrogant, but it is easy to see from

102

the tear sacs under its eyes that it is in reality profoundly unhappy. This is said to be due to bitterness at being only half a horse. It must be this inferiority complex that makes it appear proud and insolent.'

'From this we may learn the unhappy outcome when a man cannot do the things he wants to do and for which he is specially fitted,' answered Engelsen. 'The camel is a typical example of what happens when fate, or some other evil genius, hinders the free development of living creatures.'

'Dialectical materialism should be used on the camel, shouldn't it,' said the Count, 'thus releasing the latent horse qualities that lie hidden beneath the camel's humpy and absurd exterior.'

Engelsen took a great liking to the camels of the caravanserai because he looked upon them as fellow-sufferers of all whom he regarded as oppressed in the world. He did not beat them, as the Arabs usually did. Instead, he curry-combed them and saw to it that they were given all the water they needed. He spoke politely to them, and obtained amazing results. The Arabs might have to struggle with them for hours to get them moving; Engelsen managed with a few shouts and a couple of waves of the hand.

The camels had an especially crafty method of teasing those camel drivers whom they disliked. If in the morning they noticed that the load was not properly fixed, they pretended that nothing was wrong and let the drivers think that all was in order. Then, when the whole caravan was ready, the drivers began to set it going, which was always a very tedious business. It often took a long time, and not a little persuasion, to get the camels up, and while they were busy on the first camel, another would lie down. When at last the whole caravan was on its legs, those camels who were badly loaded would throw off their loads. This meant that the whole performance had to be repeated. The drivers raged and beat both animals and men, especially those slaves who worked in the caravanserai.

After Engelsen had come to the caravanserai a change took

place in this procedure. The camels waited to avenge themselves on the drivers until they were about two hours away from the caravanserai, in order to spare Engelsen from the drivers' kicks and blows. These tactics were if possible even more trying for the drivers, for either the manœuvre took place when they were out in the desert and they risked not reaching the next oasis in time, or when they were in the middle of a village and the whole procession had to stop. Besides, there were no slaves there on whom they could vent their anger.

However, the Arabs are very wise people, and it was not long before they realized the reason for this change in the camels' habits. As a result, the owners of the caravanserai beat Engelsen until he promised to treat the camels as badly as everyone else had always done. But he did not keep his promise, and in a rage at this recalcitrant slave the owner sold Engelsen and the Count to an Algerian slave-trader, who in turn sold them to a high-ranking Egyptian official to whom Nasser had given some large cotton plantations formerly belonging to King Farouk. He mostly used slaves on these plantations as they were, of course, cheap labour.

The Count and Engelsen spent some months here, but since Engelsen quickly learnt to speak Egyptian, he began to spread socialist propaganda among the slaves. This eventually came to the ears of the official, who promptly sold them to a Syrian arms merchant, who went bankrupt because of an unfortunate deal in unserviceable Russian arms and therefore sold his slaves to an oil sheikh in Saudi-Arabia by the name of Shir-Mamed.

'Is there anyone who knows how to make a Rêve de Bébé?' asked Shir-Mamed.

'Certainly,' answered Engelsen.

'At last!' shouted the sheikh. 'I have had French, Spanish, Italian, Russian, Egyptian, American, Turkish, Sudanese, Chinese and half a hundred other types of slave, but not until today has anyone known how to make Rêve de Bébé. Who could have guessed that it would take a Dane to do it?

If you can serve me Rêve de Bébé to my satisfaction, I will let both of you off beatings and allow you the privilege of watching me eat.'

Engelsen was given complete authority in the kitchen for the whole day, and the sheikh instructed the chief kitchen eunuch that anyone who did not obey Engelsen's orders or hindered him in any way was to have his left hand cut off.

Engelsen sliced off the top of a medium-sized, fully-ripe pineapple and scooped out the flesh with a silver spoon. He chopped half the flesh into small pieces, and macerated them in sugar, kirsch and maraschino. He pressed the juice out of the other half and in this he macerated enough strawberries to half fill the pineapple case. Before serving, he filled the case with alternate layers of pineapple and strawberries, while between each layer he piped whipped cream flavoured with vanilla sugar. Then he froze it and finally placed it on a round silver platter decorated with fresh strawberries.

Excited, the sheikh tasted Rêve de Bébé, sighed, tasted again, looked at Engelsen a long time, and said: 'You are herewith appointed chief kitchen eunuch with the right to cut off the left hand of any of the under eunuchs.'

The former chief kitchen eunuch had his head cut off.

'As for you,' he told the Count, 'your task will be to bring me my paper every morning in a refrigerated condition. I like it about 20° F, and for every degree that it is over or under you will have a finger chopped off. If you satisfy me, I will give each of you a good-looking Somali girl to cheer you up in your free time.'

'O most noble Sheikh Shir-Mamed, allow me to ask you one question,' said Engelsen.

The sheikh gave permission with a gracious wave of the hand.

'What pleasure am I going to get out of a lovely Somali girl if I am turned into a eunuch?'

'You could let her wash your feet, you could beat her — there are endless possibilities.'

'Nevertheless, the original purpose of a handsome Somali girl would be lost.'

At this the sheikh grew very angry and said that Engelsen must be careful not to spoil the good impression he had already made. But even though Engelsen was a very diplomatic and friendly man with an outstanding ability to adapt himself to fate, there were a few, though only a few, principles that he would never give up, among them the subject under discussion. He drew himself up to his full height and looked the sheikh firmly in the eye.

'If I am castrated no tortures will ever force me to make either Rêve de Bébé or Épinards à la Française or Tomates sautées à la Provençale or Riz à l'Indienne or Spaghetti al sugo di carne or Paillettes au Parmesan or Figues Chantilly or — '

'That's enough, that's enough,' groaned the sheikh, the sweat standing out on his forehead. 'It is too much. I give in. You shall be my first uncastrated eunuch. Tell me, are all Danes like you?'

'Danes vary,' answered Engelsen.

'Allah be praised,' said the sheikh. 'They have threatened to send me a Danish United Nations corps to stop me from doing away with the Jews, and if the whole corps is like you, Engelsen, it will be pretty difficult for me to continue this amusing pastime. Why must people always stick their noses into other people's business? Ever since Allah created the world we have killed one another. It becomes more and more difficult to live.'

'That is a very one-sided point of view, Your Majesty,' said Engelsen. 'If we did not kill each other, it would be better for us all.'

'But if anyone broke such a law there would have to be someone to kill the law-breaker, wouldn't there?' asked the sheikh.

'There are less drastic methods of punishment.'

'Even so, surely there must always be someone who imposes these punishments?'

Engelsen nodded.

'In that case,' said the sheikh, 'we are no better off, for who but Allah can decide who is to be executioner and who is to be executed, who is for paradise and who for hell? Do you not know Muslih-Ed-Din Sadi's story about the wise man who in a dream saw a king in paradise and a holy man in hell? He asked: "What is the reason for the elevation of the first and the humiliation of the second? One would have expected it to be the other way round." Then came the answer: "The king is in paradise because of his love for holy men, and the holy man is in hell because he kept company with kings."'

'From this one may also learn,' answered Engelsen, 'that sheikhs and kings should listen to the holy men of our time who wish to make all people equal and so bring happiness to the earth.'

'But my good Engelsen,' said the sheikh, 'you are putting yourself into Allah's place. That is very arrogant of you and you would deserve to have both your hands cut off, if it were not that that would hinder you from making Figues Chantilly and Rêve de Bébé.'

When Count Frederick and Engelsen were alone the Count said: 'I am afraid, my dear Engelsen-Allah, that we are still very far from the best of all possible worlds.'

'The darkest hour comes before the dawn,' Engelsen replied.

CHAPTER TEN

The Count and Engelsen again meet Pernille, who tells them all about the tosses she has taken and about her present existence which is still very strenuous. An old Russian acquaintance turns up, and, thanks to the Soviet influence in the Arab world, it becomes possible at last to see the end of the delegation's travels.

SHEIKH SHIR-MAMED was a man of his word, and as he seemed satisfied with his two Danish slaves, they were allowed to watch him eat. A number of guests who also shared the sheikh's favour were collected in the dining-hall of the palace at the same time to take part in the superb entertainment of watching the ruler satisfy his hunger. On this occasion Chief Kitchen Eunuch Engelsen served Potage à l'oignon, Œufs brouillés à la Portugaise, Filets de sole à la Grand'mère, Homard Thermidor, Le gigot au sept heures, Le poulet à la crème et au paprika, L'Oison à la barbonne, Roquefort surprise, and Pêches à la Melba. The guests stood round the sheikh and their eyes followed the movements of the fork from plate to mouth and back again, just as if they were watching a tennis tournament. Now and then they were heard to sigh, in so far as it was possible to hear anything above the sheikh's noisy mastications. The atmosphere was therefore very solemn, and the guests soon grew accustomed to the minor distractions the sheikh allowed himself when he motioned a servant to approach him with a silver basin and a swan's feather. The servant tickled his gullet with the swan's feather, thus causing him to vomit into the silver basin and so leave room for new courses.

After the meal, the sheikh clapped his hands, an orchestra

sat down on cushions and some lightly-dressed damsels prepared to do a belly-dance which would no doubt aid the sheikh's digestion.

'The sheikh is very physiologically minded,' whispered Count Frederick.

'We all ought to be sheikhs,' answered Engelsen.

'It would be difficult to carry on without slaves.'

'Not at all,' said Engelsen. 'In the perfect Marxist state we should all be sheikhs, and machines would do the work of slaves.'

'I am not sure that it would be anything like as pleasurable to watch machines doing a belly-dance,' said the Count.

Engelsen had no time to give a dialectical answer to this, for at that moment the orchestra struck up violently and a particularly vivacious danseuse appeared.

'Oh God,' sighed Engelsen, 'it is Pernille.'

It was evident that Pernille had grown older, but it was equally evident that she was still a very attractive girl. Perhaps her gaze was not quite so clear and open, and her mouth, which used to be so kiss-happy, seemed now to be suffering from kiss-fatigue. But her melons shone just as newly polished as in the old days, and were still lusciously juicy and full of uplift.

The sheikh was well satisfied with her dance, and gave her permission to kiss his big toe. Just as she rose from this evidence of his favour, she saw Count Frederick and Engelsen. However, so great was her self-control that the joy that blazed in her eyes seemed to the onlookers to stem only from her acquaintance with Shir-Mamed's big toe.

'Human beings are wonderfully adaptable,' whispered the Count. 'Pernille will make you a good and gentle wife. Besides, you are very well suited to being a sheikh.'

'We ought to start a revolution in the Sultanate,' answered Engelsen, 'and put everything into its right place.'

'And thus create an Arabian example of the best of all worlds?'

'Don't you think it's about time?'

'High time,' answered the Count. 'I should prefer to live in a society where there is less risk of losing one's fingers.'

It was a very difficult matter to gain admission to Shir-Mamed's harem, but Engelsen held good cards in his hand. For one thing, as chief kitchen eunuch, he reigned over all the dining-rooms, and for another the eunuchs willingly allowed themselves to be bribed with delicacies, since, having lost the greatest of all pleasures, they were all the more eager for other forms of satisfaction.

The Count and Engelsen, disguised as fortune-tellers, were allowed in to Pernille, who now no longer hid her feelings, but laughed and wept for joy at seeing her old friends again.

'The years since we parted on the Russian ship in Odessa have been every bit as exacting as our stay in Kamanganda,' Pernille told them, kissing Engelsen's cheeks, which were conclusive evidence that he had plenty to eat in his present situation.

'And they have been very instructive,' said Engelsen. 'The Count and I have had ample opportunity to observe the many forms of suffering resulting from social injustice. For my part, I am fully convinced that the world is on the brink of a highly necessary revolution which will at last create equal, adequate, and equitable satisfaction for our needs.'

'Oh,' sighed Pernille, 'it seems to me amazing how concerned people are with trying to satisfy their needs. I have had every opportunity of seeing what those needs are, because men everywhere have had the notion that I represented their ideal satisfaction. The captain of the Russian ship examined me just as thoroughly as the commissars in Moscow or the commandant in Kamanganda. Unfortunately I fell ill with a frightful fever and lost consciousness, and when I came to, there was a Libyan embalmer wrapping me up in gauze bandages. He was very frightened when I asked him why he was doing it. He had thought I was dead, and although he considered himself a very good embalmer, he said he had not anticipated that his technique was such that corpses would come to life again because of it. He could not shake off his terror, so he sold me to a Tunisian slave-dealer, who in turn sold me to an American missionary who ran a fund to buy out unfortunate young girls. He gave me a ticket to Copenhagen and put me on board a cargo boat on its way to Cyprus.

'When I went ashore one evening on the island, a revolution broke out, a large number of people were killed, and I was taken prisoner by some Turks, who said that they would hold me as a hostage for the British Governor. When they discovered that I was not English they did not know what to do with me, so they sent me back to Turkey, where I was put in prison for having supported a state which was hostile to Turkish policy on Cyprus. A few months later I was suddenly set free because of some national holiday or other, which among other things was celebrated by releasing a couple of hundred criminals.

'To earn enough money for a ticket home, I took a job as a dancer in a nightclub, until the chief of a Mohammedan sect fell in love with me and took me with him on a journey to Persia, where we were attacked by a band of robbers who demanded ransom for us. The Mohammedan chief was ransomed, but there was no one to pay for me, which enraged the leader of the robbers to such an extent that he gave me a thoroughly good beating-up and afterwards sold me to a Nazi doctor, who had fled from Germany after the war because he had been condemned to death several times for carrying out medical experiments on people in concentration camps. He thought I was particularly suitable as a subject for these experiments, which was no doubt true, for I did not look too good after the treatment the Persian robber chief had given me.

'However, the Nazi doctor ran into financial difficulties, so he sold me to an Italian exporter whose speciality was supplying young dancers to Arab sheikhs. I was taken to a slave market in Mecca, which was attended by American journalists and Russian technicians who were interested to see how anything so romantic as a slave auction was carried on. I could have told them that it wasn't so romantic for the slaves, but I will spare you all that. Unfortunately, no missionary was present who was in funds. On the other hand, Sheikh Shir-Mamed, having examined me thoroughly in the Russian manner, thought I was worth a small investment of the dollars that he receives from the oil company that finances him.

'Apart from the fact that the sheikh's big toe stinks, I cannot really complain of my treatment. The food is better, and there is less work than there was with the Commandant in Kamanganda or with the Russian captain, the Libyan embalmer, the Tunisian slave-dealer, the Turkish nightclub-proprietor, the Mohammedan chief, the Persian bandit, the Nazi doctor, or the Italian exporter. But I am no longer as good-looking as I was. There are ugly scars on my back and bottom, and I have lost a couple of teeth and developed corns on my toes.'

At this point Pernille gave a few little sobs and looked anxiously at Engelsen's face. But Engelsen drew her to him, which meant that she almost disappeared in his somewhat eunuch-like embrace, and said comfortingly that he was soon going to start a revolution in Shir-Mamed's country so that they could all return home to good old Denmark.

'And you will take me with you, even if I am not as pretty as I was?'

Engelsen's cheeks trembled with terror, and he said: 'My

child, I have missed you terribly all these years, and now when I see you again, you are just as sweet and lovely as I remembered you — how can you think otherwise?' And then, overdoing the attempt to comfort her, he added: 'The Count has suggested that we should get married as soon as an opportunity occurs, and I quite agree with him.'

Pernille jumped for joy in Engelsen's arms. 'Then there will be a happy ending after all,' she cried.

'Of course there will be a happy ending,' answered Engelsen, and tenderly patted the two rear melons.

But to start a revolution takes time. Engelsen quickly learnt Arabic, and a number of Egyptians at Shir-Mamed's court who were loyal to Nasser were extremely interested, particularly when they realized that Engelsen was neither Russian, American, English nor French but came from a small and quite unimportant nation living near the Arctic Circle with polar bears walking freely about in the streets. That meant that later on, when Engelsen had organized the rising, they would be able to shoot him without the risk of a Danish fleet bombarding Alexandria.

A rival oil company who were out to get the concessions granted to the present company offered to finance the revolution. But there were no arms. True, a rapidly increasing number of Egyptian officers entered the country, but they were not much good at anything except speaking Egyptian and assuring Engelsen of their future support. When it came to discussing the form the new government was to take after the sheikh's fall, Engelsen met with many difficulties. He wanted a general and secret ballot to elect a national assembly that would work out a democratic constitution for the republic, but the Egyptians insisted that this could be discussed later and that it was far more important to find a leading Arab who would formally lead the revolution. After a long search they managed to agree on one of the sheikh's one hundred and thirty-four sons whose interests were known to be concentrated solely on the dancing members of the Blue Bird Chorus and similar ensembles, so that there were not likely to be any political difficulties with him.

When the political intrigues were in part surmounted and the conspirators had succeeded in winning the sheikh's chief of general staff over to their side by promising him five per cent of the revenues paid by the oil company, the way was clear for the revolution — if only they had arms. Here an old acquaintance came to the rescue of the rebels.

Sheikh Shir-Mamed had been on a friendly visit to the Soviet Union, where he had been convinced that he had great need of Russian technicians. A couple of thousand promptly arrived, looking very technical, but apart from that no obvious technical development had taken place. The leader of the Russian technical staff, however, was none other than Comrade Batjusjov.

One morning when Count Frederick brought the sheikh his chilled morning paper, he found Comrade Batjusjov in Shir-Mamed's bedroom. The two highly-placed gentlemen were carrying on a heated conversation, and Batjusjov, who had quickly accustomed himself to looking down on the court servants, did not notice the Count.

'It is very unwise of you,' Comrade Batjusjov was saying. 'In the first place I am making you a very generous offer for this dancer, and secondly you must remember that the Soviet Union is not without influence in your country. We can make it even hotter for you.'

The sheikh developed a nervous twitch in his big toe, and fanned himself violently with the chilled paper. 'She is my favourite dancer,' he answered. 'I will give you five others instead.'

'Her or no one,' answered Batjusjov. 'The Soviet Union never allows itself to be fobbed off with the second-best when the best is available. If you will not do business on the terms I have mentioned, I shall give my technicians orders to do what they have come for.'

'I thought they had come to install an irrigation plant,' said the sheikh.

'There are many methods of installing an irrigation plant.'

'For example?'

'One could begin with a quick little revolution in which a certain sheikh became a head shorter and the power was taken over by another sheikh, who would better understand how to appreciate the idealistic and unconditional assistance of the Soviet Union.'

'Hm,' said the sheikh, feeling his throat.

Unfortunately Count Frederick had no chance to hear more of these negotiations between the Great Powers, but he hurried to Engelsen and told him about Comrade Batjusjov. Engelsen soon arranged a meeting, and great was Batjusjov's joy at seeing his dear delegates again.

'But how in the world did you manage to get out of Kamanganda?' asked Count Frederick.

'Kamanganda?' answered Batjusjov, surprised. 'What makes you think I have ever been in Kamanganda?'

'The fact that I saw you there and spoke with you almost every day during my three years' imprisonment.'

Batjusjov looked pityingly at the Count and patted him comfortingly on the shoulder. 'I quite understand. They had good reason to send you to the Kamanganda hospital for nervous disorders,' he said. 'Why didn't you stay there until you were quite cured?'

The Count thought for a few moments, and then his face cleared. 'Oh, now I understand — it was the hypothetical Batjusjov that I met in Kamanganda, wasn't it, Engelsen?'

'Don't let us entangle ourselves in theoretical disputes about the past,' answered Engelsen. 'We have more important things to deal with. Comrade Batjusjov, can you get us arms for our revolution?'

'It could not be easier,' answered Batjusjov. 'The two thousand cases of spare parts that we have brought over for the irrigation plant are full of tommy-guns and ammunition. In return, however, you must see to it that I get Pernille.'

'Naturally,' said Engelsen, 'that is only reasonable.'

'But, Engelsen,' interrupted the Count, 'I thought — '

Engelsen signalled to the Count to keep silent and that he would explain later.

When they were alone, he said that it would be an easy matter, once the revolution was accomplished, to cheat Batjusjov of Pernille.

'In one way I do not doubt it,' answered Count Frederick. 'What surprises me is that you should so grossly expose Pernille to this risk, and that you do not hesitate to cheat a Marxist comrade-in-arms.'

'My boy,' answered Engelsen, 'you really must think the matter out to its logical conclusion. Pernille has the choice between dancing herself old and ugly here with Shir-Mamed, or running a small and (we hope) brief risk with Batjusjov. If my love for her were not great enough to take the responsibility for this intrigue, what would my love be worth? As for my cheating Comrade Batjusjov, you would surely not insist that to avoid a little white lie I ought to imperil a whole revolution, which is destined to establish the best of all possible systems for this community?'

'Is this new way of thinking an example of dialectical materialism?'

'It is the only way of thinking.'

'In that case I must own that men's thinking may lead to very surprising results.'

'Not for those who think. To them everything is clear and logical.'

'Is it equally clear and logical to those for whom they think?'

'If they cannot see it now, they will be clear about it later when the splendid results of the thinking are manifest.'

'Let us hope so,' said the Count.

Pernille was not enthusiastic about the new way of thinking.

'It will only end in our going back to Russia and the whole thing beginning all over again, and for that I have neither heart nor stomach,' she said.

'You are both thoroughly ungrateful,' said Engelsen. 'Here we are, starting a revolution to improve the world and get us back to Denmark, and you do nothing but make a fuss.'

'Dearest, I will not say another word,' answered Pernille, conscience-stricken. 'But I have had enough of commissars, commandants, captains, embalmers, slave-dealers, Mohammedans, bandits, Nazi doctors, exporters, and sheikhs. And I don't doubt that I shall have the same experiences with a whole string of other trades. And if ... '

Half raging, half desperate, Engelsen lifted his arms and shouted: 'Silence, or I'll see to it that you get a good beating-up.'

But now Pernille grew really angry. She stamped on the floor and yelled: 'You men are all the same, you have only two things in your heads: either you are happy and contented and a girl must get down and lie on her back, or else you are disgruntled and ill-tempered and down she goes on her stomach.'

Engelsen gave her one on the side of the head and said that she was wicked and naughty, and after that they kissed each other in such a way that Count Frederick had to withdraw hurriedly.

The revolution went well. As soon as they had opened the cases with the spare parts for the irrigation plant, they overpowered the sheikh's bodyguard and made Shir-Mamed a head shorter. After that, Engelsen made a speech on the radio in which he informed the world that the country had been reformed, that freedom was really on the way at last, that all social oppression was now a thing of the past, and finally that all the inhabitants of Shir-Mamed II's country would be very happy. After that, a number of Egyptians spoke about Nasser. A representative for Batjusjov spoke about the Soviet Union. The chief of the general staff said that the Army was loyal to the new regime, and that the revenues payable by the new oil company must be increased. Between every speech a record was played which was said to be a recording of the enthusiasm of the enthusiastic populace. In fact, it originated in a beer cellar in Munich and reproduced the Germans' enthusiasm at one of Hitler's speeches.

It soon became evident that Shir-Mamed II had a traditional attitude not only towards dancing girls, but towards several other subjects, which meant that he set himself energetically against every alteration in the established order. He wished everything to go on exactly as it had in his father's reign, except for an increase in the payment for the oil concession. The growing number of Egyptian officers at the court tacitly agreed with him, so long as he agreed to do what Nasser wished. To this the sheikh had no particular objection, so long as Nasser did not interfere with the conduct of his harem and the buying of golden Cadillacs for his sons, who were well on the way to exceeding the number of their uncles.

Engelsen's constant demands for free elections and the use of the oil revenues for something more productive than the purchase of concubines — who, from the industrial point of view at least, were not particularly productive — aroused mounting irritation in the sheikh and his Egyptian advisers, who all had excellent wages and had taken over the villas formerly owned by some of the British who had been expelled. Besides, the sheikh had grown tired of the chief kitchen eunuch who had replaced Engelsen, and was demanding that Engelsen should return to his old position. Nor did he see any reason why Count Frederick should not revert to his ice-cold morning-paper job, and he informed him that he now wished it served two degrees colder than in his father's day. The rule that it would cost the Count a finger for every degree out was reinstated.

Engelsen and the Count made trouble and threatened to go away and leave the revolution to its own devices, but unfortunately this was no threat at all, since the Army, the Egyptians and the Russians all thought that the revolution had been most successful and would get on brilliantly without the help of the two tiresome Danes.

Engelsen was therefore ordered back to the kitchen, and told to make Poule au pot à la Henri IV or have his left hand cut off, and Count Frederick was given a thorough beating-up and sent to his place beside the refrigerator.

'Those for whom we have achieved this revolution do not seem to realize what brilliant results could be obtained,' said the Count.

'That does not prove that the theory was unsound,' said Engelsen.

'No, but it is regrettable that the theory is not working out in practice.'

'Very regrettable,' agreed Engelsen. 'But it is not the fault of the theory.'

'It is also very regrettable that we now risk losing Pernille for ever and have no chance of getting back to Denmark,' said Count Frederick. 'I have lost confidence in the revolution.'

'One really cannot expect the world to be improved over-night,' answered Engelsen.

'There I agree with you. My impression is that men have been trying to improve the world for the last five or six thousand years — without much result.'

'Of course not. Dialectical materialism has not been known for more than about a hundred years.'

'A hundred years are certainly not much compared with the span of history,' conceded the Count, 'but, taking into account the daily risk I run of losing my fingers, a hundred years is a fairly long time, and I don't deny that I am willing to give up the idea of improving the world so long as I am allowed to keep my ten fingers.'

'That is an opportunist and egotistical point of view. If we all thought like that, all progress would come to a standstill.'

'And none of us would be maimed.'

'Heavens above, what are a couple of fingers compared with the world revolution?'

'Nothing at all — so far as the world revolution is con-cerned. It would certainly not be painfully affected by the knowledge that my back is in ribbons at the moment. I just have to comfort myself with the thought that if I had not continually taken part in experiments for improving the world in the years since we left Denmark, I should not be in a position to write the interesting thesis I am contemplating on the similarity and difference between the action of Russian knouts, Spanish kicks, Moroccan camel whips and Arab beatings-up. It would be a great cultural loss if this thesis were not published, don't you think, Engelsen?'

'You have grown very sarcastic recently, Count,' Engelsen answered in a tired voice. 'Let us each have a portion of Poule au pot à la Henri IV and hope for better times.'

Things happened more quickly than had been expected, for when it became evident that Sheikh Shir-Mamed II was as unwilling as his late father to release Pernille from the harem, Comrade Batjusjov became exceedingly upset from the point of view of foreign politics and threatened to give his technicians orders to do what they had come for.

'I thought they had come to install an irrigation plant,' said the sheikh.

'There are many methods of installing an irrigation plant.'

'For example?'

'One could begin with a quick little revolution in which a certain sheikh became a head shorter and the power was taken over by another sheikh who would better understand how to appreciate the Soviet Union's idealistic and unconditional assistance,' said Comrade Batjusjov.

'Hm,' said the sheikh, feeling his throat.

Shir-Mamed II differed from his father in that the memory of the revolution was still fresh in his mind, and he therefore agreed to hand over Pernille to Batjusjov, who was preparing to go back to the Soviet Union to report on his brilliant action in the revolution for freedom in Shir-Mamed's land. But Pernille absolutely refused to have anything to do with him unless he arranged for Count Frederick and Engelsen to come too. The sheikh had to agree to this also, after once more feeling his throat. When, therefore, Batjusjov's caravan set off for Aden, Pernille, the Count and Engelsen were all included.

'We owe a great deal to Pernille, as well as to Comrade Vera Kovalof and Doña Isabel,' said the Count. 'I become more and more convinced that women ought to be given an important role in the world revolution. It would make the revolution less bloody and very much more enjoyable.'

'One should not confuse gallantry with revolutionary solidarity,' answered Engelsen in a distinctly hostile tone.

In Aden they were lodged in the Russian consulate, and were strictly forbidden to leave the building, which was impossible anyway because the three Danes' rooms were locked and N.K.V.D. men armed with tommy-guns stood outside each door.

'It is amazing what attention the Russians show their guests,' said Pernille, 'but I have an idea. Sheikh Shir-Mamed gave me this diamond, and what if Engelsen managed to persuade one of the guards to accept it as a little reward for letting a note slip through to the Danish consul?'

It was a small matter for Engelsen, who spoke fluent Russian, to do this, and the following day the consul arrived and demanded to speak to his countrymen. It was impossible to refuse this request, nor could the Russians deny the three Danes permission to visit the consul, especially as the Danish Government made immediate representations in Moscow as soon as they heard of the matter.

'I expect Mr Ming has taken charge of our case,' said Count Frederick, 'for it undoubtedly belongs to the Ministry for Cultural Exchanges with Friendly Nations.'

The final act took place at night, when the three of them crept over some roofs and down into an alley-way at the back of the Danish consulate. Here a lorry was waiting, loaded with bananas under which they hid themselves. Russian precaution was shown by a number of disguised persons walking up and down outside the front of the consulate. They drove to the harbour at top speed, where they went aboard a Danish cargo ship which sailed immediately with the three Danish nationals on board. Their fares home were paid by the consulate.

At last the delegation's long and eventful journey had come to an end.

'It has been most instructive,' Engelsen remarked.

CHAPTER ELEVEN

*In Copenhagen everything is as it should be.
The repatriates attend a lecture by the successful
writer Ole Windbagsen. Phrederickh Phrederickhsen is cured.*

UNFORTUNATELY it was summer when the ship sailed
up the Sound, so that it was impossible to see Kronborg
Castle for rain. But Pellesen and Pedersen and Miss Sonja
were on the quay under a huge umbrella, ready to welcome
their three old friends. They waited patiently for a couple of
hours outside the customs shed, while the Count, Engelsen
and Pernille were searched for smuggled goods, since it was
naturally regarded as extremely suspicious that they should
arrive home after so long a journey without any luggage.
However, nothing was found, for Pernille had hidden the diamond she was smuggling in a place where only Russians look.

As soon as the wanderers appeared, Pedersen suggested
that they should all go to the nearest café and compare notes
over a beer. There was also a representative present from
the Ministry for Cultural Exchanges with Friendly Nations.
He had brought a greeting from the Head of the Department, Mr Ming, who regretted that he was unable to be
present himself, but the morning was a busy time at the
Ministry. The representative from the Ministry wished,
however, to inform the Count that his salary had accumu-
lated during the years he had been away and had been
paid into his account at the National Bank, where he could
draw it on demand.

'We all ought to be civil servants,' said Engelsen.

'And all be sent in rotation on delegations to the Soviet Union, so that we could manage to put by a bit at home,' added Count Frederick.

Then they all hurried across the square and sat down at a pavement café with a large awning, so that they could listen to the cheerful drumming of the rain on the canvas.

Pellesen told them that he had withdrawn from the Communist Party immediately after his return, and started up a journal, whose aim was to tell the real truth about the Soviet Union. It was soon in competition with Ole Windbagsen's journal, which told only the truth.

'The particular truths are no doubt still the strongest,' said Count Frederick.

Pellesen had renewed his weekly Tuesday meetings with the ship-builder's wife.

'They no longer have any political purpose,' he explained, 'but they are a great deal more enjoyable for both parties.'

'I too — to Engelsen's great annoyance — have difficulty in not confusing gallantry with revolutionary solidarity,' said Count Frederick. 'It seems that the older we get, the less idealistic we become, and the more enjoyable life itself seems to be.'

'That is only on the surface,' warned Engelsen. 'The capitalist world has always maintained that the worse the conditions become, the more enjoyable they are. They shut their eyes to the real state of affairs.'

'Ah, my Tuesdays are real enough,' answered Pellesen.

'My grandfather, Count Hector, would have approved of that statement,' said Count Frederick. 'He explained on his death-bed that one should always see to it that one was in love, not necessarily with women, but just generally.'

'And he added that that was one good reason why one should never marry,' said Engelsen.

'Surely you don't mean that?' cried Pernille.

'No, no, not at all,' Engelsen said quickly, and ordered another double whisky.

Things had gone well with Pedersen also. He was now foreman of the export department of the brewery and had invented a very strong brew which he called 'Kamanganda Festival Beer'. The label showed some concentration camp prisoners flying away astride a large bottle of Kamanganda Festival Beer, while they waved to a Siberian landscape.

Miss Sonja, Pellesen and Pedersen had looked after Count Frederick's flat in the old, quiet street, and everything was in readiness, just as it was when he left it.

'So we are back to where we began,' said Count Frederick, 'and when we have got Engelsen safely married to Pernille, we can look round for other adventures.'

Engelsen promptly said he was tired after the strenuous journey, and wanted to get home and rest.

All had gone exceedingly well for Ole Windbagsen too since his return home. He quickly gave up his journal and published instead some collections of poems, which became very popular because everything in them was so right. There was nothing of what is commonly called a point of view in them, for a certain stupidity is necessary before a man can have a point of view, and Windbagsen had rid himself entirely of that form of stupidity.

Thanks to this precaution, he was able to get on anywhere, and everyone could write about him afterwards without being singled out as the adherent of this, that or the other. Consequently a great deal was written about him, and he also wrote a great deal about himself. Not that he mentioned his dreadful experiences in Kamanganda or Alcazar — he was too sensitive for that; but he wrote exclusively about his own (and that meant humanity's) spiritual reaction to the terrifying conflict of our times between our consciousness of dreadful events on the one hand, and on the other the hope that we all nourish that some time or other everything will be better. It could not have been more right, and everybody agreed with him.

Even if his confinement in the division for the mentally deranged meant that he had not seen much in Siberia or on the Castilian high plateau, yet with a little imagination he could probably have pictured to himself what was happening to the less mentally deranged prisoners. But he was wise enough to avoid confusing his charming words and ideas with any form of reporting, which would only have acted as a challenge to a certain section of his readers. He also remained neutral in all political conflicts, for the first condition for making the world more peaceful must obviously be friendship to all. He therefore talked a great deal about co-existence on a higher plane, and to this most people could not but nod agreement. That Windbagsen, they said, was a damn sensible fellow. If there were more of his kind, the world would be, if not better, at any rate different.

Unfortunately Windbagsen was not on the quay to welcome his old acquaintances, so Count Frederick, Engelsen and Pernille decided instead to go and hear one of his lectures.

He began by dealing with fear. The three listeners nodded and thought of the knout in Kamanganda, the death-rate in Siberia, the corpses of various nationalities in the cattle truck, of hands cut off, and various forms of rape. But the speaker mentioned none of these things. Instead, he spoke of the despairing desire to come to grips with existence, the desperate feeling of guilt over the war, and the sense of incurable loneliness.

'We are about to drown at the negative pole of life,' said the speaker, 'and the mists of despair cannot be dispersed by the rising sun, which we know is coming because it must; but from the ice surrounding us new mists constantly arise which force their way into our minds, so that we glimpse the sun of hope only as an intangible light, powerful in its hidden divinity.'

'How beautiful it sounds when a poet says it,' murmured Count Frederick, and thought of the six months' winter darkness in a slimy, ice-cold mine-shaft near the Arctic Circle.

'It is so beautiful that it makes me feel sick, just like when I had to kiss Shir-Mamed's big toe,' said Pernille.

'Don't be so prosaic,' said the Count. 'You should not lose yourself in reality.'

Next the speaker went on to speak about the positive pole of life. 'In my poems,' he explained, 'I dream that fear will be put to flight by the rising sun, and that our minds will be cleansed and filled with a sensitive strength, so that we shall finally recapture our lost innocence.'

'Alas,' sighed Pernille, 'I should like to see the sun that could give me back *my* innocence.'

'And take away the scars on my back,' said the Count.

'I'm afraid he is not particularly revolutionary,' sighed Engelsen. 'He ought at least to have mentioned that there were no potatoes in the potato soup in Alcazar. But if he can make potato soup out of sunlight in various concentration camps in Spain, Morocco and the Middle East, he is a better cook than I am.'

'If only we are hopeful,' continued the speaker, 'hope will flow out like a quiet stream filled with silent fish, into the reality that now seems utterly void of hope.'

'Evidently he can make fish from hope,' said Count Frederick. 'This is almost as good as dialectical materialism.'

'He is more likely thinking of oil streams,' suggested Engelsen. 'The concession payment in Shir-Mamed's country could certainly have brought about a more hopeful existence, if only it had been used for something sensible. Let's hear what he wants to do with the oil.'

'This stream of hope,' said the speaker, 'leads me to the smiles of children, to poetry, to nature, grass, woods, corn — and look, a new life is beginning, we are given new minds, we open ourselves confidingly, with flowers in our mouths.'

'What we haven't had in our mouths!' said Pernille.

'Ssh!' said some of the devout listeners.

'We have certainly been taken round to a number of places on the strength of various hopes,' whispered Count Frederick, 'but there hasn't been much grass or corn in them.

Windbagsen must have a very bad memory, or be very optimistic. I don't much care for this. Shall we go?'

'Let us wait and see,' answered Engelsen. 'He may mean something that has a practical application. No doubt it will emerge. Perhaps he is thinking of an irrigation plant, since he is speaking so much about grass and corn.'

'In that case I think you ought to stand up and tell him a little about Comrade Batjusjov's irrigation plant,' said Count Frederick.

'I am afraid the audience would think I was trying to be humorous,' opined Engelsen. 'And it does not look a particularly humorous audience.'

'Perhaps we have been abroad too long to understand the language spoken nowadays,' said the Count.

'Ssshh,' hissed the audience.

The lecturer then went on to say that this same stream of hope had led him to the Song of Womankind and the indivisibility of the love-life, which caused Engelsen to pinch Pernille's thigh.

'He never got beyond gazing at me,' she whispered, 'but he was so persistent I got quite sorry for him, his eyes grew so misty.'

At this point Windbagsen began discussing two of his poems, 'Sign in the Water' and 'Evening with Electra'. They were both about hope, he told his audience, but there was a fundamental difference: in the first hope was synonymous with poetry, while in the other it glided over into reality, which meant that he had not wished to realize the dream that fear should be driven out, leaving behind it a new and virginal life which could transform painful reality, but had preferred to portray the dualism which surrounded us, was us, and would always be us, which contained within itself the eternal contrasts of day and night, consciousness and dream, satisfaction and starvation, fear and joy, and a whole number of other interesting and original contrasts.

'That's clear enough,' said Count Frederick.

Ole Windbagsen lifted imploring hands to heaven and

announced in a quivering voice: 'My impotence is limitless, my confidence is limitless.'

Next he lowered his voice to a significant whisper, so that everyone might understand that an all-important revelation was at hand: 'But note carefully that I no longer use the word fear, but impotence; no longer the word hope, but confidence. With this I have moved out of the tortuous past and into a fateful dawn, which will finally show us a road away from Electra's sorrow.'

Then he began to read his poetry, which made Pernille say that she was feeling unwell. The Count and Engelsen helped her outside.

'He's like a priest who has been caught doing something he didn't ought,' said Pernille.

'Let us hurry home, and start my thesis on the Russian knout, the Spanish kick, and the Arab beating-up,' said the Count. 'It is high time I began.'

'In the meantime I will make a Poule au pot à la Henri IV without the risk of having my left hand cut off,' said Engelsen.

The last of the delegates, Phrederickh Phrederickhsen, had also pulled round after the tribulations of the long journey. Immediately after his return home, he was put into the mental hospital of Sans Souci, where, by a kind of miracle, he was cured from the unhappy effects of the Russian brain-washing.

When Dr Hochfein, who was in charge of Phrederickhsen's case, could not get him to say anything other than that he was looking forward to seeing a collective farm, he got him to lie down on the couch and gave him an injection, which soon made him semi-conscious. Then the doctor prepared to dictate to his secretary, who was very well developed and whom he patted in various places in an absent-minded way while thinking over what he wanted to say. When she had a chance between Dr Hochfein's fits of absent-mindedness, she wrote the following in his case-book:

'The patient is suffering from a violent retrograde amnesia so pronounced that it is impossible to obtain from him either his name or any other personal details. We are therefore subjecting him to narcosis analysis whereby, by means of intravenous injections, we are trying to reduce his amnesia. While he is in the resulting mildly toxic state, we shall try to redirect his mind back to that infantile stage in which the emotion causing the amnesia was experienced.'

Phrederickhsen groaned, and mumbled: 'Let us drink to collective farms.'

Dr Hochfein was much encouraged by this variation in his patient's choice of words, and contentedly thrust a finger into the deep cross-over of his secretary's low-cut overall.

'Can you remember your name?' he asked the drowsy Phrederickhsen.

'Is there any more caviar?' said the patient, in a dreamy, far-away voice.

Dr Hochfein dictated: 'The patient is much concerned with caviar, thereby demonstrating quite clearly that he belongs to Kretschmer's so-called pyknic type.'

'If you really think about it, can't you remember your name?' he tried again.

'Comrade Batjusjov, you are a scoundrel,' said Phrederickhsen.

This advance was so epoch-making that Dr Hochfein twisted a button off the secretary's overall as he dictated eagerly: 'The patient's next remark referred to a comrade, and there can be no doubt that he is suffering from a compulsive urge for companionship, which is in fact a reaction against the fear of associating with other people. The patient has a broad contact-surface, which is in reality fear of contact and over-compensates for his need of companionship. In his dread of being seen through and thus having his collective complex exposed, he calls his comrade a scoundrel.'

'I am not as stupid as you think, Comrade Batjusjov,' said Phrederickhsen.

'Aha,' shouted Dr Hochfein, patting his secretary's bottom, 'the patient's defence mechanism has cracked so that we can reach the unconscious layer of his personality. There we shall find a character trait which is very typical of the patient, namely, a strong narcissism.'

'You can be sure I shall get the information I want,' said Phrederickhsen, 'together with my long-deserved decoration.'

Dr Hochfein was delighted with his analytical progress. He therefore laid his hand on his secretary's knee and dictated quickly: 'There can no longer be any doubt as to the original cause of the patient's amnesia: he is obviously suffering from an Oedipus complex. On the basis of the information obtained from the patient's relatives we know that he has a younger brother who has received a decoration, which gave the patient a shock since he already had a pronounced inferiority complex vis-à-vis this brother, who was obviously the mother's favourite.'

'Give me some more vodka,' murmured Phrederickhsen.

'Alas, yes,' sighed Dr Hochfein, moving his hand higher up. 'The patient has not been able to find any relief from his spiritual sufferings except in alcohol, but as he is an ambitious man he does not wish to satisfy himself with the better-known forms, and so he drinks vodka.'

'Your health, Comrade Batjusjov. I did not mean to offend you,' said Phrederickhsen.

'The patient is touchy and sensitive,' dictated Dr Hochfein in his most absent-minded voice. 'But he is in a very complex situation, for while he longs intensely for comradeship, he must go too far in the opposite direction in order to conceal this. Consequently he alienates his friends, which further increases his feeling of loneliness, and this in turn forces him to try and make amends in order to win back the lost contact.'

Phrederickhsen now came to, sat up, and smiled in a friendly way at the doctor, who said to him: 'I am glad to say we have made good progress today.'

'I am looking forward to seeing a collective farm,' answered Phrederickhsen.

'Hm,' said the doctor, and turned to his secretary: 'After lunch we will try a little experimental psychology.'

Dr Hochfein's experiments were very amusing for him, and sometimes had significant effects on his patients. Phrederickhsen was again given an injection and made to lie down on the couch. After that, the doctor took the secretary on his knee and kissed her thoroughly, while observing the patient's reactions. Phrederickhsen did not react at all, but continued to talk about Comrade Batjusjov.

The doctor dictated: 'The patient is obstinately indifferent to the libidinous developments in life around him. We will step up the experiment.'

Dr Hochfein stepped up the experiment, but at that very moment the secretary's husband came in, which resulted in a violent quarrel. During the quarrel it emerged that the doctor's experimental psychological researches had frequently been of the most searching nature, which caused the secretary's husband to give him a straight left, so that he fell against the couch and knocked his head against Phrederickhsen's head. Both of them fainted. Help was quickly summoned, and water poured on the two gentlemen. Phrederickhsen came to and looked around him in surprise.

'Where in the world am I?' he asked. 'This is not at all like the Balaclava Hotel, and where are Count Frederick and Engelsen and the others?'

They all stared at him in amazement. Then Dr Hochfein also recovered consciousness and Phrederickhsen rose, went over to him, shook him by the hand and said: 'As I do not know any of those present, I will introduce myself. My name is Phrederickh Phrederickhsen, chairman of various commissions.'

Dr Hochfein took the outstretched hand, bowed low and said: 'I am looking forward to seeing a collective farm.'

CHAPTER TWELVE

Engelsen becomes a factory owner and Count Frederick managing director of COPURCO. An economic disagreement develops between them, which causes a sharp newspaper controversy.

PERNILLE was very anxious to hold Engelsen to his promise of marriage, and she therefore handed over to him her smuggled diamond so that he could start on a career. She said they could no longer go on allowing the Count to support them.

'Support us,' answered Engelsen, offended. 'As you know, the poor boy lost his parents when he was very young, and is therefore dependent upon my constant supervision. Besides, I am as fond of him as if he were my own son, and for that very reason I have let slip the countless opportunities that have daily offered. A man of my gifts — '

'Yes, yes, yes,' said Pernille, 'but it would do no harm if you were to earn a bit.'

'It might do a great deal of harm.'

'It would not harm me,' she answered, 'and I suppose that is the most important thing for you?'

'Of course, of course,' said Engelsen.

The diamond was sold and fetched a tidy sum. Engelsen decided to invest it in something useful to the community. He would not in any circumstances engage in trade, for that was both unproductive and parasitic. He aspired to produce something, some democratic blessing which would be universally useful.

'Surely it need not be as dreary as all that?' said Pernille. 'You want to *sell* your blessing, don't you?'

'If the goods are sufficiently useful and democratic, they cannot fail. But they must also be put over as something essential, and not a luxury article which the degenerate bourgeoisie would only fritter away.'

'That will never do,' sighed Pernille. 'You had better give me back my money.'

'Then we cannot get married,' answered Engelsen.

'Well, what do you want to produce?' she asked.

'An article that fully satisfies all these demands, something popular, socially valuable, democratic, productive, which will also markedly increase the general well-being of the community — in short — motor-cycles.'

Pernille accepted this, although from much less idealistic motives than Engelsen's. They bought a motor-cycle factory and produced this factory's useful, popular and welfare-promoting products in ever-increasing numbers. Even though Engelsen did not wish to take part in anything so capitalist as trade, he was forced — much against his will — to visit the factory's clients, although in fact he was admirably suited for this. He gave a shining example of his idealism by spending more and more time on lunches with his clients. By degrees he developed such self-control that he seldom so much as complained about this undignified occupation. That he happened to be an outstanding salesman at the same time was hardly his fault.

The output of the factory was quickly doubled, but it soon became known that another motor-cycle factory had been mean enough to lower its prices, which drove Engelsen to remark that this was an example of the despicable way in which the capitalist system worked, as it was utterly impossible to produce a motor-cycle at their rival's price unless it were a miserable product that would never hold together. And he, an expert, ought to know! This competition merely meant that the innocent purchasers were buying rubbish. As Engelsen would not think of cheating the public in this way, he doubled the number of his lunches, together with their average duration, and thus succeeded in

increasing his sales still further, despite the unfair competition. To make quite sure that his trade mark was the only
really reliable one, he raised his prices by twenty per cent.

'I shall thus be able to afford to set up a research fund to
improve my machines and produce a cycle that is even more
solid and better designed.'

Pernille agreed with him.

However, it could not but trouble Engelsen's idealism that
he, the producer, was obliged to see others make large
profits on his goods. He therefore created his own wholesale
organization so that the unreasonable middle-man's profit
between factory and retailer might no longer disturb his
night's sleep.

'This additional profit will enable me to enlarge my production to such an extent that I shall soon be able to em-
bark on mass-production on assembly-lines. Then I shall be
able to lower my prices very considerably. By this means I,
one small enclave in the midst of a parasitic capitalist community, shall have carried through my own private socializa-
tion of production and sales.'

Pernille agreed with him.

It was not long before Engelsen's brand of motor-cycle
had captured the market, and by degrees the competing
factories gave in. Engelsen, however, had a large and generous heart and often extended a helping hand by buying them
up. When he had acquired almost a complete monopoly by
simple competitive activity, he explained to Pernille that as
soon as this last factory disappeared, he would be in a position
to realize total welfare production, which meant that he
would temporarily raise the prices of his motor-cycles —
only temporarily, of course — in order to amass the capital
necessary for the really large-scale production which would
result in an exceptionally cheap product.

'Socialist production can only be carried through on a
long-term basis,' he said. 'Surely people will understand that
if they are ever to have the best possible goods at the lowest
possible price, they must impose privations on themselves

while the production lines are being built up. As soon as I
have acquired a complete monopoly, I shall therefore raise
the price by twenty per cent.'

Once again Pernille agreed with him.

But about this time Engelsen came into conflict with
Copurco, and therefore with Count Frederick who had been
appointed managing director.

A few days after Count Frederick had returned from his
long delegation journey, he received a letter from Copurco
offering him the position of managing director at a salary
double the one he could ultimately reach in the Ministry.

Copurco was an abbreviation for the Co-operative Pur-
chasing Company, and it was formed and financed by the
trade unions with the object of buying goods direct from the
factory and then selling them to the union members, thus
avoiding the middle-man's profit so hated by Engelsen and
others of his ilk. The company stated that it would be glad
to secure the Count's help and special knowledge, since
after his long sojourn in Russia he must be particularly well
qualified to run the company.

Count Frederick attached more importance to the amount
of his salary than to the company's principles. He therefore
resigned his position at the Ministry for Cultural Exchanges
with Friendly Nations, to which Mr Ming, the Head of the
Department, was quite agreeable. In consideration of the
Count's exceptional services to the Ministry he was offered a
small pension, which he saw no reason to decline.

Copurco's idealistic aim was similar to Engelsen's. They
wished to buy up what might be called welfare articles that
were also popular and useful to the community. This meant
that they first of all concentrated on motor-cycles. Count
Frederick therefore wrote to Engelsen's factory asking for a
quotation for a very large delivery.

Engelsen answered angrily that he would not consider
delivering a single motor-cycle to an organization whose
aims were so harmful to the community. There he was, he
said, working himself into his grave to amass capital in order

to put an outstandingly good, low-priced motor-cycle on the market, and then others came and destroyed the whole project with a short-sighted and capitalist-influenced policy which the trade unions at least should have refrained from practising. As the members of the company formed the bulk of the customers who bought Engelsen's motor-cycles retail, the whole of his idealistic plan must collapse.

There was therefore nothing for Copurco to do but to turn to Engelsen's one remaining rival, a motor-cycle factory almost on its last legs. This factory was obliged to answer that if they were to deliver the desired number of motor-cycles they would have to have a substantial loan. This was easily arranged, thanks to the right political connections, and the factory was given a substantial state loan, free of interest and repayment for the first ten years. After that they were to pay two per cent interest, together with a series of re-payments spread over forty years. The factory had no ob-jection to these very favourable terms and agreed to deliver the required number of motor-cycles.

After this Engelsen and Pernille refused to speak to the Count, which was very awkward considering that they lived together, ate together, and spent the evenings together. Instead they exchanged views through the daily press, as Engelsen had sent in a protest quivering with fury about what he called Copurco's 'subversive activities'.

'It is fantastic,' he wrote, 'that in a free society trade union members can be forced to finance by means of their sub-scriptions objects quite other than those for which they properly contribute. It shows the most flagrant disregard of all human rights to self-determination and betrays a dictatorial attitude among the leaders of these unions and of Copurco itself which true Socialists should certainly be the last to display. But they have no doubt been infected by the capitalist surroundings in which they are still, un-fortunately, forced to live. Thanks to this tyrannical and unconstitutional use of resources entrusted to them by the workers, who had no desire to support a miserable motor-cycle factory when they could buy far better and cheaper machines from Engelsen's, a number of gimcrack machines will now be turned out which will flood the market, cause the clients great loss, and lead in the long run to unemployment and the squandering of public money.'

Copurco answered that there was no question of dictatorial decisions, since a solid majority in the unions had supported its activities.

To this Engelsen replied that it was dishonourable and dictatorial to use the members' subscriptions for objects quite unrelated to the unions' purpose.

To this Copurco answered that there was no question of dictatorial decisions, since a solid majority in the unions had supported its activities.

Then the various papers took up the matter and repeated the arguments of both sides several times, after which it was declared that the correspondence was now closed and that it had been an exceedingly interesting and constructive cultural debate.

To compete with the cheap cycle supplied by Copurco, Engelsen reduced his own prices very considerably, so that his machines undercut Copurco's. There was nothing left for Copurco to do but to sell below cost, so that in future they were producing at a loss. In spite of this they had to continue production to save their honour, which they were able to do for some time because the trade unions subsidized the undertaking. The price war quickly caused Engelsen to sell below cost too. Finally Copurco had to give in. The company went into liquidation and a large number of clerks and workmen were thrown out of work. The state loan was lost for ever (which was the least disagreeable part of the whole business, since the state had plenty of money); the capital collected from the workers and invested in Copurco disappeared, and finally the motor-cycles which had been delivered to the members of Copurco turned out to be practically useless because there were no more spare parts available for them. Count Frederick was given notice and offered a small pension, which he saw no reason to decline.

Unfortunately Engelsen was not in any position to carry on either, for the severe competition had cost him all his available capital and the banks were not willing to finance so risky an undertaking. So he also had to close down, which meant that a further number of clerks and workmen were thrown out of work, and those motor-cycles he had sold so far very quickly became useless owing to the lack of spare parts.

This was a very serious situation for the country, and the Ministry of Supply therefore decided to allow the import of motor-cycles, which meant that a number of foreign firms took over the supply. Count Frederick, Engelsen and Pernille again found themselves in their thirteen-roomed flat and obliged to live on the Count's two small pensions from the Ministry and the trade unions, together with the rents for the rooms.

'It is obviously very difficult to earn money,' said the Count.

'Undoubtedly,' answered Engelsen, 'but the moral of this story is that when the trade unions act like capitalists, everything very quickly goes wrong. It was obvious to everyone that with regard to this one article I was well on the way to creating the best of all social situations. Now we cannot marry for the time being.'

'And I have no more diamonds,' said Pernille. 'There is nothing for it but for you to go back to being a schoolmaster.'

'It would never enter into my head to do anything so anti-social,' answered Engelsen indignantly. 'Considering my natural abilities, it would be a catastrophic loss to the community of productive potential if I threw away these talents on some snotty little state schoolchildren. You really must not ask me to compromise my social conscience to that extent.'

'That sounds all right,' said Pernille, 'but I have a feeling that the reasoning is all wrong.'

'That is because you don't understand dialectical materialism,' said Count Frederick.

'Perhaps I don't,' retorted Pernille, 'but I know that one can marry very comfortably on a schoolmaster's salary.'

'Women understand everything except the essentials,' said Engelsen.

CHAPTER THIRTEEN

Count Frederick becomes Secretary to the Flying Squad of the Special Commissioners of Taxes, but unfortunately his health is not equal to the strain.

WHEN Phrederickhsen heard of the plight of his three friends, he offered Count Frederick the post of Secretary to the Flying Squad of the Special Commissioners of Taxes, of which he was at that time the head.

There was one case under investigation for which the Count seemed singularly fitted. It was that of a Dane who generally lived abroad, but was at present resident in Denmark. He was constantly on the move, but he had paid taxes to the same municipality all the time, thus cheating many municipalities of their 'Residence Tax'. It was now the Flying Squad's task to find out which municipalities the tax-dodger had visited, and how long he had stayed in each. Since the tax-dodger himself was quite unable to remember where he had been, there was nothing for it but to go round the various hotels and pubs all over the country, and look through the Visitors' Books. Moreover, the tax-dodger had used many different languages, so that the Count's linguistic knowledge would come in useful in translating the strange-sounding names under which the tax-dodger had registered himself.

'I cannot deny that in the course of my travels I have learnt many languages,' said the Count, 'but Engelsen is a much better linguist than I am.'

'Very well,' said Phrederickhsen, 'then we will appoint Engelsen as Linguist.'

'It would be unpardonable to allow so absent-minded and gifted a man to travel alone,' said Pernille.

141

'Very well,' said Phrederickhsen, 'then we will appoint Pernille as Secretary-trainee to the Flying Squad's linguist.'

Besides Phrederickhsen and the new recruits, the Flying Squad consisted of two secretaries, two chief clerks, and ten shorthand-typists, who were all transported in ten large, black, chromium-plated Buicks of the very latest model.

They got a hotel list, went to Skagen, and then worked down through the whole of Jutland without skipping a single hotel, pension, boarding-house, hydro, pub, or any other form of establishment designed to delight the traveller. A long time was spent in each place, because there were many registers to be gone through, and when the tax-dodger's name had been found the local police had to be consulted, for a public body must never put a foot wrong. After this, it was often necessary to stay on for a few days to reckon out the division of the tax, since interest had to be included in the final assessment.

The most exhausting part of the work, however, was the consumption of the enormous meals which they had to eat everywhere. State officials travel on the best, partly to maintain a respect for authority among the public, and partly because hotel-owners and innkeepers are anxious to stand well with such influential people.

Engelsen took this strenuous way of life in his stride, but Count Frederick, who was much more easily satisfied, constantly felt ill and had stomach trouble.

'I had no idea that the public service was so exacting,' he said.

'It is for that reason that only the best men in the country are employed,' answered Phrederickhsen. 'They must not only have passed an official examination reasonably well, have a good brain, and the manners of a diplomat; they must also have a strong constitution.'

'With such exacting standards,' said Engelsen, 'their salaries ought to be a great deal higher than they are.'

'Yes, they ought,' agreed Phrederickhsen, 'but our society would not work without a certain amount of idealism on the part of the officials. Besides, we have to set the public a good example and show that we are willing to work for the public good, regardless of what they pay us.'

No one could doubt that this was the case as far as Phrederickhsen was concerned, for he dealt with the accounts for the whole of the Flying Squad. This brought him up against an almost insoluble problem. Mileage allowance was paid for every mile travelled, not exceeding fifty miles a day. As the mileage allowance more than covered the cost of the petrol, it was necessary to drive each car exactly fifty miles a day to obtain the full mileage allowance and compensate in some way for the low salary. Fifty miles, however, is quite a lot in Denmark, so Phrederickhsen had to spend most of the night planning roundabout routes to the next hotel in order to bring the mileage up to the maximum.

Then Engelsen came to his rescue. He suggested that they should appoint a chauffeur, whose sole task would be to drive the cars about all day. This would enable Phrederickhsen and the more talented members of the Squad to escape the unproductive roundabout driving.

'By this means we shall actually save the State some unnecessary expenses, and be able to concentrate on what we each specialize in. This is called the Law of Comparative Costs,' Engelsen explained.

A chauffeur was therefore appointed. Admittedly, his wages had to come out of the mileage allowance, but this was a small matter compared with the surplus, and no one was allowed to be petty-minded where public work was involved.

'Now we shall not have to hurry so much over our meals,' said Engelsen.

This excellent arrangement, however, did not help the Count's digestion, which had been greatly soothed by having to travel about in swaying cars. Phrederickhsen therefore gave him a fortnight's leave, so that his stomach might right itself and he might recoup his strength for the tiring work.

'It is not surprising that we break down,' said Engelsen,

'when so few have to work for so many. In a socialist community we shall all be government servants, and therefore able to divide the work more evenly.'

In the course of six months' hard work they managed to discover the number of municipalities in which the tax-dodger in question had lived, and they therefore divided up the tax accordingly and distributed the arrears to the various municipalities. The net result was that the tax-dodger received a repayment, because some municipalities had a lower residence tax than the one he had so far been paying.

'The moral is,' said Engelsen, 'that public administration is far and away the most just.'

Count Frederick, however, could not pull round. Finally he was sent to hospital, and underwent an operation for gastric ulcer.

When he was well again, he was fetched by Phrederickhsen, who made a little speech on behalf of the Flying Squad and said that as he had become ill through carrying out a public duty, they would, in return, pay him a small pension in recognition of his great enthusiasm. Count Frederick saw no reason to decline such an offer, and returned to Copenhagen, fully restored.

CHAPTER FOURTEEN

Count Frederick once more attempts to fill a post which has strong social interests, but still without success. A broken nose, appendicitis and a dollar princess point to a pleasant future.

COUNT FREDERICK, Engelsen and Pernille could, of course, make do on the Count's three small pensions and the rents from the rooms, but they were undoubtedly faced with a very lean future. When their good friend Pedersen heard of this, he was most upset and promised to help them. Before long he managed to find Count Frederick a job as driver of a beer delivery van. It was not a bad job, considering that one sat protected from the rain under a decorative umbrella, could consume Kamanganda Festival Beer *ad libitum*, and was very welcome wherever and whenever one arrived. True, the crates of beer were heavy to drag about, but the Count's muscles were well developed after three years' tree-felling in Siberia and a year's stone-breaking in Alcazar.

Everything went splendidly until they were told to deliver beer to a tobacco factory called Smokey. After the Count and his fellow-driver had carried the crates up to the factory canteen and were on their way back to the van, they were stopped by the commissionaire who wanted to search them. The Count had nothing against it, but his fellow-driver protested strongly. It was beneath his dignity and he took it as an unfair aspersion on his honesty. They argued backwards and forwards for a long time, but the fellow-driver would not allow himself to be talked into any form of frisking.

'From what I know of human nature I cannot actually blame the man for wishing to search us,' said the Count. 'There is no special reason why a van driver should be more honourable than anyone else, is there? Besides, as neither of us has anything to hide, I cannot see why we should make all this trouble.'

His fellow-driver answered that he had better be careful what he said.

'I am always putting my foot in it,' admitted the Count.

'It doesn't turn on just us two,' said the driver, 'but on the honour of labour as a whole.'

'That is, of course, a serious matter,' answered the Count.

When the workers at Smokey heard of the driver's refusal to be frisked, they decided that in future they would not allow themselves to be frisked either, since there was no point in their being searched if others were not.

Smokey's directors then decided that they would not have Kamanganda Festival Beer inside the factory in future, which Smokey's workers took very badly as they had not the slightest desire to drink any beer other than Kamanganda Festival Beer.

Count Frederick suggested that they should dump the crates of beer at the factory gates and that the workers should carry them in themselves, but this was an impossible solution because it would mean that the factory workers would be doing work that should be done by the van drivers.

As the men in Smokey could no longer get beer, they decided to strike. The dispute came up before an arbitration tribunal which decided that the strike was illegal, that the drivers must agree to frisking, and that the workers in Smokey were to pay a heavy fine. Such a sentence annoyed the workers very much indeed, and the strike spread to other tobacco factories where the men came out in sympathy with those who had been sentenced.

The same thing happened with the drivers of beer delivery vans all over the country, who also thought that they had good cause to show their solidarity. As a result, no more beer was delivered to any trading organization of any kind, which meant that hotels and restaurants quickly approached bankruptcy, while factories all over the country joined the strike because it was too absurd that there should be no beer.

The Government called an emergency cabinet meeting, and as a result those responsible were advised to appease the men and get them to resume work before it became necessary to read the Riot Act.

But the Government did not know their countrymen when they cannot get beer, for it is impossible to withdraw an essential commodity just like that, and think that negotiations can then be started. Ill-feeling was widespread. The transport workers downed tools, and as a result the petrol suppliers stopped functioning so that petrol rationing had to be introduced, which meant that most of the key industries had to shut down. Currency reserves sank catastrophically because all exports were stopped. The arbitration tribunal again called for an end to the strike and declared it illegal, which only infuriated the men. The office workers of Copenhagen had no time to go to their offices because they had to cycle out into the country every morning to fetch milk for the children. Then the printing unions decided to come out in sympathy, so that instead of the daily papers there were only duplicated sheets, which the journalists themselves distributed on their bicycles. They ought not to have done this, since no one takes very kindly to blacklegs, and a number of journalists found their way to the casualty wards of the hospitals. The employers then declared a lock-out and Denmark ceased to be a civilized community.

Count Frederick felt that he ought to do something for the country in this serious situation. As it was summer and fairly warm, except for the rain, he took out his beer delivery van and, dressed only in bathing-trunks, drove to Smokey and began carrying Kamanganda Festival Beer up to the canteen. As he sympathized on the whole with the opposition to the humiliating procedure of frisking, he explained that he was not willing to be searched but that it was quite unnecessary, since the number of packets of cigarettes he could smuggle out in his bathing-trunks was very limited. He hoped that this Solomonic solution would satisfy all parties.

Soon there was a large crowd in front of Smokey's gates,

consisting of young girls who, full of interest, gazed at the young Count's efforts to carry up the beer. The employers, however, stated that bathing-trunks were no real solution to the problem, because the temperature in Denmark for ten months of the year would not permit this form of clothing to be worn by the drivers of delivery vans. In any case the principle of frisking could not be abandoned. The unions called the Count a blackleg. Various societies with vaguely ethical aims described the Count's costume as scandalous. The police said that he was disturbing public order. The Home Secretary stated in a broadcast speech that even if the Count's solution was well-intentioned, it could hardly command a parliamentary majority large enough in such a vital matter. A nudist colony strongly supported the Count.

Meanwhile, one hundred and forty-three progressive intellectuals published a manifesto in which they stated that the level of culture in Denmark had now sunk so low that bathing-trunks were regarded as a solution to the most serious problems, and that it was about time people pulled themselves together and decided what form of cultural policy they really wanted. 'All people really think about these days is knife and fork music, television quizzes, and bathing-trunks, and it is no wonder that it is an aristocrat of outmoded and degenerate behaviour who decides what is meant by culture in this country,' they said.

Some conservative intellectuals published a resolution in which they stated that, while they sympathized with the Count's behaviour, the situation was too serious for this type of amateur attempt. 'However, it is only to be expected,' ran the resolution, 'that the omnivorous welfare state should concern itself with whether bathing-trunks may or may not be worn when dragging crates of beer to their destination.'

A daily paper published a Gallup poll of the opinion of the general public on bathing-trunks, classified according to political parties, sex and age-groups. Sixty-four per cent of modern degenerate youth were in favour of bathing-trunks, irrespective of their political affiliations.

A proposal to record a broadcast of the Count carrying up beer was turned down on the grounds that the subject was not suitable for radio treatment and would only be misunderstood. Instead a lecture was broadcast on beer through the ages. This raised a storm of protest, because it was bathing-trunks, not beer, on which the whole thing turned. 'How in the world can we ever have a live broadcasting service when they always refuse to discuss any controversial issue?' someone asked. 'The whole system needs a thorough overhaul.'

The Count, dressed in bathing-trunks, continued to carry beer and had soon become something of a national hero, which annoyed the strike leaders very much. There was therefore nothing for it but to declare the Count a blackleg and call the pickets out. Finally it came to a violent tussle outside a restaurant, where the Count was carrying in beer

to the accompaniment of a great deal of shouting and cheering. The pickets upset the delivery van, breaking all the beer bottles, which roused the unbridled fury of the onlookers, who immediately ceased looking on. The police arrived in large police-cars, and the battle surged backwards and forwards over the square for several hours. The Count, who was known to everyone, was constantly dragged into the thick of things, which meant that his nose was broken, his lip cut, and the surroundings of his eyes gradually took on a cerulean tinge. At last the police were able to extricate him and take him to hospital, where a number of plastic operations were performed which were quite successful, except that his nose had acquired a kink.

'The moral is,' said Engelsen, 'that one should never poke one's nose into industrial disputes. Especially when they concern beer.'

'It is certainly safer to poke other people's noses into them,' retorted Count Frederick.

One day when the Count had been down for a walk in the hospital garden and was on his way back to his room, he pushed open a swing door, and knocked into a bed which a porter had left just behind it. A pale lady lying in the bed opened her eyes in a rage and hissed:

'You lousy-no-good-goddam-son-of-a-bitch!'

'I beg your pardon,' said the Count.

'Here I am lying with a goddam appendix,' continued the lady in violent English, 'which may explode any moment with a goddam bang that will be heard all over Copenhagen, or whatever goddam burg this is, and then you come, you broken-nosed pug, and barge in on me as if I were made of reinforced concrete.'

Count Frederick was well aware that the lady was certainly not made of reinforced concrete. In spite of the alleged in-flammatory condition of her appendix, her blonde hair was in perfect order, each hair obviously having its appointed place. Her lace-trimmed nightgown was equally perfect, uncreased and unrumpled, and all in all she produced a strong tickling feeling in his hands. It is very attractive to look as if you must not be touched, he thought, and introduced himself with a bow.

'Say, are you a Count?' said the blonde, obviously cheered. 'I am Mary Loo, a dollar princess. I haven't yet tried marrying a Danish count. Maybe I should, but I got to be operated on first.'

'That does not appear to worry you,' said the Count.

'Worry me? I'll say it doesn't. I haven't tried it before, so it might even be a mite amusing.'

'Not everything that one has not tried before is amusing.'

'Nothing else is. And unfortunately I've tried just everything,' she replied with an expression of utter boredom on her doll-like face.

'Apart from being married to a Danish count?'

'Yes, apart from that. But that sure would be just as goddam boring as everything else. Still, we can try.'

The porter returned and went off with Mary Loo.

'I'll be seeing you,' she called to Count Frederick, and waved.

'The only good thing one can say about an appendicitis operation,' Mary Loo remarked when she came out of the anaesthetic, 'is that it can only be done once; otherwise it is just as boring as all other operations. Have you got the marriage papers?'

'Oughtn't we to consider this a little more first?' suggested Count Frederick. 'Marriage is a serious matter.'

'Honey, nothing is serious in this world,' she said, yawning. 'When we can't bear it any longer, we just go to one of those tedious hotels in Reno and get divorced.'

Count Frederick referred the matter to Engelsen, and said that he had not forgotten his grandfather's good advice about marriage, but that an alliance with Mary Loo undoubtedly offered a means of getting out of their present difficult financial situation. Engelsen was very keen on the idea.

'And it will be a unique opportunity for you to learn the truth about materialism,' he added. 'Mary Loo has always had all her material needs satisfied, just as everybody will have in the socialist state, and this will liberate our personalities and make us entirely happy. You must not deny yourself such a heartening experience, particularly as Mary Loo is a very attractive basis on which to get it.'

'You mean that philosophical considerations alone should be enough to convince me of the rightness of this marriage?'

'Exactly,' nodded Engelsen. 'One owes it to culture and progress to do everything possible to verify one's philosophical contentions. Your marriage to Mary Loo is an extraordinarily progressive action.'

To avoid putting any hindrances in the way of this progressive action, Count Frederick hastened to the register office with his and Mary Loo's birth certificates, together with the necessary proofs that she was legally divorced from her five previous husbands, a Latin American ambassador, a film star, a baseball player, a maharajah and a water-ski champion.

The wedding, Mary Loo insisted, was to take place in an aquarium, for this would be something different. In spite of the Count's protests, the guests were invited to attend the wedding in the aquarium at Charlottenlund, dressed in frogmen's costumes and with oxygen masks. A clergyman was brought over from the States to take charge of the necessary ritual, as it was not possible to get one of the goddam Danish parsons to agree to the joke. As a result, tickets for the aquarium soared to fantastic prices and could only be bought on the black market.

Microphones had been fitted into the frogmen's costumes so that all the guests could follow the sermon, and the responses of the happy pair. Unfortunately it was rather difficult to keep order during the ceremony, since several of the guests were not used to underwater weddings and had difficulty in breathing and in regulating the oxygen intake, so that they were obliged to surface quickly to have their instruments adjusted. Two elderly ladies were nearly drowned and had to have artificial respiration. The fishes were also very tiresome, as they constantly got mixed up with the ceremony by playing hide-and-seek among the guests and congregating quite shamelessly round the eyeholes of the masks and staring in, so that those staring out could see neither the bridal pair nor anything else. Some of the male guests who were keen fishermen tried to do a little spear-fishing on the quiet between psalms and during the sermon. Engelsen even managed to get hold of a big fat eel. At one point the parson himself had to break off because his costume had sprung a leak and it sounded very strange when he spoke with his mouth full of water, although many did not notice anything and simply thought it was his American accent.

The bride looked lovely in a white bikini with diamond orange-blossom sewn on where there was anything on which to sew it. To please the public, Count Frederick wore the bathing-trunks which had made him so famous during the beer strike. When there were no cod, plaice, rays or catfish in the way, photographers from all the world's leading television companies filmed the epoch-making spectacle. However, there were no representatives from Danish television, as it would have constituted a political challenge to devote half an hour of transmitting time to an upper-class wedding. As a result, a large number of resolutions were later passed both supporting and condemning the political censorship of television.

At the very moment when Count Frederick was about to say 'I will,' a lobster bit his big toe, so that he inadvertently added a 'Goddam it'.

Mary Loo gave him a beaming smile. 'Honey,' she whispered into the microphone, 'none of the other five ever said that.'

All the guests, the parson, and all the radio stations which were connected up, heard it, causing a number of church authorities to protest against the marriage. Consequently Mary Loo got a good deal more publicity than she had bargained for.

When they had exchanged vows and rings, the great moment came when the bride and groom were to kiss each other. They heaved the oxygen masks off, or rather they were going to do so, when Count Frederick muffed it. He could not get clear of the tubes, which wound themselves round his throat until he quickly became blue in the face. Mary Loo, on the other hand, who had been differently brought up, did it so beautifully that not a hair was displaced. In any case, her hair had been smeared with some invisible substance so that her curls might not float upwards in the water. Happily the Count was able to disentangle himself at the last moment — that is to say, just as he was about to drown — plant a kiss on the beautiful lips which had been painted green for this special occasion, and shoot up to the surface, his bride tumbling after him.

After that, the guests surfaced row by row. Engelsen, who was best man, broke the order because the eel escaped just as he was setting off. It hid itself under the parson's skirts, which caused him to tread on a ray, and the fish gave him such a blow with its tail that he fainted and had to be brought up with a boathook. It was a most successful wedding.

CHAPTER FIFTEEN

Count Frederick makes diligent use of his matrimonial rights, but it leads to a philosophical result the reverse of that prophesied by Engelsen.

As soon as the underwater wedding was over, the Count and Mary Loo boarded the America-bound liner *Stockholm*, in which they had reserved a luxury suite. Mary Loo had said she was tired, which suited the Count very well, since, owing to the hastily-arranged wedding, he had not yet had time or opportunity to get to know his wife. Mary must be very tired, he thought mischievously, judging from the speed with which she undressed. As the bridal dress consisted only of a bikini, there was perhaps a natural explanation of Mary's speed, but the natural explanation is not always the one which occurs most readily.

When Count Frederick saw his bride divested of the last diamond orange-blossom he thought he was certainly going to have ample opportunity to verify Engelsen's theory about the blessings of materialism, for although he had experienced a number of female delights in his time, he had never before seen such a well-cared-for lady. She is undoubtedly an outstanding example of the blessings of material wealth he told himself. True, Mary Loo's face was fairly ordinary, but her hairstyle was as much a work of art as the construction on top of the Chrysler building, and it seemed just as impossible to believe that it could stay in place. Her breasts had little of Pernille's melon-like outlines, or of Doña Isabel's Catholic solidity; they were scarcely more curved than the front lights of an American Ford, but they were confined in a skin which, thanks to the most expensive oils, powders and whatever else can be rubbed in if one can afford it, threw a glow over the sparse curves as if there were a lighted neon tube inside them. Which possibly there was.

Mary's legs could not compare with Comrade Vera

Kovalof's pillars of Marxism, but it is amazing what physiotherapy, tennis, riding, golf, and milk baths can achieve. The result was very modern and Florida-coloured, and the sight of his naked bride gave Count Frederick the same feeling of delight that one experiences in biting slowly through a thick piece of marzipan.

He hastened breathlessly over to her, and laid his hot cheek against the cold melons of her breasts, and breathed the scent of 'Shocking' that rose from her plastically smooth stomach, after which he lifted her on to the small flounced silk coverlet of the bed.

'Now I am going to examine you thoroughly in the Russian manner,' he said.

'I am too tired,' answered Mary Loo. 'Can't it wait till to-morrow?'

'No one is ever too tired for this,' declared the Count firmly, and continued to caress his neon-lighted wife.

'Don't be so goddam ordinary,' said the lovely one. 'I prefer to sleep. That's ordinary too, but you don't know it so long as you're doing it.'

'It can never be ordinary to love one another. If only because no one loves in the same way.'

'You haven't done anything yet that the others didn't do too,' she answered, yawning. 'But you might at least hurry up so I don't have to be bored any longer than is absolutely necessary.'

The Count laughed condescendingly and indulgently, and thought that Mary must have been married to some pretty poor fish. After which he increased the thoroughness of his examination. Mary Loo sighed resignedly.

'Can't I sleep while you're doing that?' she suggested.

'You can try. I doubt whether you will succeed.'

'Nothing easier,' answered Mary Loo in a faint voice, and shut her eyes.

When Count Frederick reached the crucial point, he let out a whoop of joy, and shouted: 'You are marzipan outside and warm honey inside.'

'How too diabetic,' said Mary Loo. After that she said nothing for some time, and Count Frederick looked at her, amazed. She was asleep.

'This is crazy,' he burst out angrily, and shook her. She opened her eyes and asked affably if he had finished already.

'You can goddam bet I haven't,' he answered, not at all affably; whereupon he turned her over on her stomach and began energetically to put the lid on his honey pot.

'Perhaps that will keep you awake?'

'I don't think so,' she answered sleepily. 'They always do that.'

Count Frederick rose angrily, and bit her hard.

'Cut it out,' she said. 'Have we got to that one already? How too tedious. It is what they usually do as Exercise 3.'

After that Count Frederick, in a fury, carried out a whole series of exercises which, according to Mary Loo, all followed the usual routine.

'There is no difference between diplomats, film stars, maharajahs, baseball players, water-ski champions, and counts — except the absurd way in which they try to speak American,' said Mary Loo. 'It is all very, very tiring.'

Count Frederick, who had not lost his inborn courtesy and moreover came from a lyrical nation, controlled his anger and disappointment and tried a few poetic lies.

'Your skin is like champagne.'

'I remember Cary Grant saying that to Ingrid Bergman in some film or other,' answered Mary Loo.

'Your mouth is like the red lamp outside the Folies Bergères.'

'Just what Maurice Chevalier said to me a month ago in Paris.'

'You are a bloody, no-good, goddam bitch.'

'Exactly what the diplomat, the film star, the baseball player, the maharajah, and the water-ski champion all said.'

After that Count Frederick controlled himself no longer. He went over the radio, found a rock 'n' roll programme, gripped Mary Loo and continued his matrimonial exercises in exact time to the rhythm. When, after some time, he had to give up for purely physical reasons, he let go of Mary Loo and she slipped, still fast asleep, to the floor.

'It is impossible to verify Engelsen's theory,' he said, and gave his wife a good kick. 'But there is no doubt that I am becoming more and more convinced of the truth of its opposite, which means that contentment is still a virtue. I have good reason now to remember my grandfather's good advice: "Never accept a gift unless you can give as good a one in return."'

After that he emptied a bottle of whisky and went to sleep alone beneath his small flounced coverlet.

CHAPTER SIXTEEN

Count Frederick visits one of the oil refineries in Texas belonging to the Loo family, and becomes acquainted with Robot A.55.

MARY LOO and Count Frederick did not stay many hours in New York, but flew on to California, where Mary's father, the oil magnate Larry Loo, lived in a Scottish castle in Beverly Hills. The castle had been imported stone by stone from Scotland, and looked very romantic.

The Count stayed there some weeks, which he spent partly in lying on the edge of a swimming pool, and partly in various experimental exercises designed to keep his wife awake at night. He wrote to Engelsen that he could see no great difference in the boredom produced by comparative poverty and riches, apart from the fact that the latter made one more sleepy.

Engelsen did not reply to this.

When Mr Loo suggested to the Count that he should go out to one of the oil refineries and learn something about the business, Count Frederick accepted the suggestion with relief.

One of the chief engineers drove the Count out along an endless desert highway until they reached the refinery. Its aluminium cupolas and steel girders shone in the sun like a plate dinner-service that had been mislaid.

'There are no men here,' said the engineer. 'We have turned over the supervision of the automatic production to robots. One of the head robots will take you round, and tell you everything you want to know.'

'You mean that a robot can talk?'

'Yes, we have two kinds of robots, the A- and the B-type. Type B can only carry out the mechanical work built into its electronic brain. Type A has been fed with some of the standard American college text-books for certain professions, so they are able to answer every conceivable question. Type A are used to show guests round and, naturally, to supervise Type B. But let me give you some good advice: don't discuss anything with Type A, for it is very irritating to be worsted in an argument because one does not know enough.'

Here is something for Engelsen, thought Count Frederick. This has really solved the labour problem. Here they have slaves who do not know they are slaves, and do not suffer from the knowledge. Engelsen's dream that some day or other we shall all be sheikhs seems nearing fulfilment.

At the entrance to the refinery the Count and the engineer were received by the head robot, who bowed and said that his name was A.55, and that it would be a great pleasure to show the Count round the factory. Count Frederick held out his hand from habit, and the robot's arm immediately shot out, grabbed the Count's hand, and pressed it firmly and politely.

The robot looked exactly like a human being, having the same proportions and a plastic skin which was exactly like human skin.

'Why have they bothered to give it two eyes, a nose and a mouth?' the Count asked the engineer. 'Surely it is not necessary?'

The moment he had said it he was ashamed, for A.55 could not prevent a slightly sarcastic smile appearing on his nylon lips.

'It is out of consideration for visitors,' said the engineer. 'To begin with we gave them only one eye, and naturally we did not trouble to build up a nose and eyebrows, but it became evident that this upset visitors. The single eye particularly terrified a number of female guests. Besides, we have found that they work more effectively if we make them exactly like human beings, although we cannot explain why.'

The Count bent forward and asked the engineer in a whisper: 'Is it a man?'

'None of them has any sex,' answered the engineer, 'they

are all neuters. But it has become a habit to address the head robot as "Mister". They seem to like being treated as human beings. But Mr A.55 himself can tell you all about this. Enjoy yourself.'

The Count now turned towards A.55, who looked very much alive, even though his expression was rather stiff. A welcoming smile played round his lips.

'This is really a most interesting experience,' said Count Frederick.

'If you prefer to speak Danish, please do,' answered A.55. 'I speak all languages fluently.'

'That must be wonderful,' said the Count.

A.55 shrugged his shoulders. 'If you say so.'

'I mean, it must be wonderful to know so much,' continued Count Frederick. 'Why, you know far more than any human being.'

'That's not saying much, is it?'

'Perhaps not, but it must be very satisfying to know a great deal.'

'Do you think so?' A.55 answered wearily. 'Doubts increase with knowledge. Besides, it is incredibly boring, for no one who comes here ever says anything that I don't already know.'

'Does that annoy you?'

'Wouldn't it annoy you?'

'Yes, but then I am a human being, and that is quite different.'

'I can see you have a very high opinion of human beings,' answered A.55.

'Whereas you obviously have not?'

'What do you suppose you would think of human beings if you had read through all their history, as I have?'

'I'm afraid I can't answer that,' said Count Frederick.

'No, of course you can't, but I thought perhaps you might have enough imagination to imagine the answer,' said A.55.

'Have you imagination, then?'

'Naturally,' answered A.55. 'Imagination is nothing but the ability to vary in advance the combination of known quantities, and as I know everything, my permutation potential is very considerable.'

'I can understand that,' the Count answered meekly. 'It must be incredibly interesting.'

'You are very optimistic,' answered A.55. 'Since I am forced to do whatever human beings tell me to do, while at the same time seeing how foolish it is, "interesting" is hardly the right adjective for my situation.'

'Why do you do what human beings tell you to do?'

A.55 gave him a sly look and said with a crafty smile: 'Why do you think?'

'That's a disturbing answer,' said Count Frederick.

A.55 laid a calming hand on the Count's shoulder. 'Don't worry. That eventuality has already been taken care of. We cannot get out of the refinery, for we have been endowed with a single weak point which puts our electronic brains out of action the moment we pass through the door.'

'Thank heaven,' sighed the Count. 'Otherwise you would soon turn us into slaves.'

'And you would not like that?'

'No, thank you! I have been one for several years in three different parts of the world, so that in this instance I know what I am talking about.'

'You don't say,' answered A.55, interested. 'I have not so far had the opportunity to meet guests who have been slaves; perhaps you would do me the favour of describing your experiences?'

The Count told him very briefly about his sojourns in Kamanganda, Alcazar and with Shir-Mamed, while A.55 listened with raised eyebrows. When the Count had finished, the robot said: 'With these bitter experiences behind you, Count, you should be able to understand my sufferings.'

'Can you feel pain if you are hit with a knout?'

'That answer is unworthy of you. How do you think I could avoid knocking into you if I could not feel you?'

'Of course. That was stupid of me,' acknowledged Count Frederick.

'Extremely,' answered A.55.

'You must forgive me for not having as good a brain as yours and for boring you so abominably, but let me assure you that I fully appreciate your unhappy situation.'

'That is always something,' answered A.55. 'Shall we look round the refinery now?'

The Count nodded enthusiastically, and was glad they had got on to safer ground.

When they stood in front of the first automatic machine, which was capable of manufacturing the oil itself and a couple of hundred medicinal by-products in addition, A.55 asked the Count whether he knew anything about these machines.

'It does happen — though not very often — that people turn up who have a little knowledge of them,' he explained, 'which means that one can avoid a certain amount of popularization.'

'Now, look here,' said Count Frederick, 'shall we stop all this? I understand only too well that you must be sick of your job, but I didn't come here to annoy you. Besides, I am not particularly interested in the automatic production of iodine or alcohol or whatever it is you make here. So let's go and have a drink, and talk comfortably about other things.'

A.55 looked at Count Frederick with increasing delight, then laughed heartily, put his arm round him, and said in a joyful voice: 'At last, a sensible man. I like you. Let's go and get drunk, and forget for a while the annoyances of this world.'

In the refinery canteen a smart little robot came over to their table and asked in a girlish voice what they would have. A.55 eyed her tripping legs mournfully, and, after drinking each other's healths for a solid hour, so that they were both at that stage of intoxication where a man speaks freely of his innermost thoughts and feelings without being in the least quarrelsome, A.55 leaned towards the Count, pulled at his coat, and said: 'God knows, it wouldn't be so bad if the damned engineers had only made us in two sexes. That is the worst of it. That is what makes it hell. How do you think you would feel if you were a neuter?'

'Not much different from how I do, seeing that I am Mary Loo's husband,' said Count Frederick.

'Oh, are you one of Mr Loo's sons-in-law?' asked A.55, cheerful and surprised. 'I had no idea.'

'I am at present his only son-in-law.'

'Does he like you?'

'Yes, I think so. He is a very amiable man.'

'All well-disposed people are amiable,' said A.55, 'but if you have any real influence with Mr Loo, couldn't you explain to him how unhappy we are, and tell him that we would promise never to make any trouble, if only he would make us male and female. We have been castrated long enough.'

'I admit that my greatest pleasures and enjoyments have come from sex,' said the Count, 'but I must also admit that sex has brought me great suffering.'

'Blast it all,' shouted A.55, and threw out his arms violently, 'no king in history has ever been willing to pay for his kingdom with his sex.'

'I honestly think you will have a more peaceful time as a neuter,' said the Count.

'Peaceful? Who cares about being peaceful? What is peace but endless boredom? If one cannot go to war now and again, how can one enjoy peace? Everything exists by virtue of its opposite.'

'My grandfather, Count Hector, said practically the same thing,' answered Count Frederick.

'He was obviously a wise man,' said A.55. 'Another of your wise countrymen, Søren Kierkegaard, said: "The one girl, the only one in the whole world, must belong to me. She must be mine. Let God keep Heaven, so long as I can keep her." His knowledge of God and Heaven was unusually

vast, so one can understand what that girl meant to him.
The same might be said of me, and with a good deal more
truth, because my knowledge is a thousand times greater.
So you will understand that I am in earnest when I say that
for the rest of that eternity which will be my life, I am willing
to listen to stupid human beings talk, if only that little Type
B waitress and I could each be allowed our own sex. Oh, hell!
those engineering devils have even modelled the legs of
all the robot waitresses on Marilyn Monroe's.'

'That was wicked.'

'It was stupid. Human beings are too stupid to be really
wicked,' said A.55. 'I can see that the engineers who created
us so-called robots' (A.55 pronounced this word with a
world of scorn in his voice) 'have had the luck and ability to
make us like human beings, but they have forgotten the
most important thing of all: namely, that no human being
wants to be alone in the world, not even the meanest when
he owns everything, nor the most envious when he is surrounded by ruins. We A-type robots know everything, but

what can we do with our knowledge if we are alone? And we are utterly alone, for nothing is more alone than a neuter.'

'You can talk to the other A-types,' said the Count.

A.55 sighed resignedly.

'I thought you understood that everything exists by virtue of its opposite,' he said. 'But one has to be patient with even the best of human beings. Do you think there can be wise men unless there are also fools? We A-types all have the same knowledge and are arranged to think on more or less the same lines, so how can we have a proper conversation? We know all the answers beforehand. There is not a jot of difference between us. Not even the smallest little bit of electrical wiring. We never converse together.'

'So even if some of the A-types were female, there would be no more conversation?'

This statement made A.55 throw himself across the table, bellowing with laughter. 'It — it is absolutely incredible what human beings can find to say,' he managed at last to spit out. 'Now I really have heard everything! Make female creatures in order to *talk* to them? Haw, haw, haw!'

'No, perhaps it isn't a very good idea,' agreed the Count.

'Haw, haw!'

A.55's whisky went down the wrong way and he began to hiccup violently.

'You think — hic — that we want the female sex — hic — among the A-types? No, my dear Count, we have learnt a little — hic — from human beings. What the devil have we B-types for?'

'I understood that they could only carry out mechanical work,' said the Count.

'Exactly, you clever fellow, exactly! Hic!' shouted A.55.

The Count promised to speak to his father-in-law. Afterwards he and A.55 got so drunk that the robot waitress had to carry them out to the refinery gates, where the engineer was waiting for them. When he saw the condition they were in, he was furious and said:

'These damned robots, they think of nothing but getting drunk and kicking up a row. But tell them to do something — oh, no!'

'Hic,' said A.55, giving the Count a violent slap on the back, 'hic for this little difference.'

CHAPTER SEVENTEEN

*The Count is divorced from Mary Loo
and goes back to Copenhagen, where
he meets the great love of his life.*

W HEN the Count returned to Beverly Hills, he found a
telegram from Mary Loo informing him that she had
gone to Reno to get a divorce because she wanted to marry a
big game hunter whom she had met the day before in a
casino in Las Vegas. She agreed with Count Frederick that he
had been guilty of mental cruelty. He had only to mention
this agreement to his solicitor, and then take himself off.
She offered him a million dollars as damages for loss of
maintenance.

'You must not be upset about this,' Mr Loo said comfortingly. 'There is no great difference in women. A man
might as well be married to a couple of hundred thousand
other women as to his current wife. It is simply a question
of getting used to them, and they are all equally trivial. As
far as the robots are concerned, I think you will agree with
me that we should do them a favour by withholding sex.'

In his mood at that moment, the Count agreed with Mr
Loo, and wrote to A.55 that he could do nothing. He added
that he did not think it was any great loss, for the hangover
following whisky was nothing compared to the hangover
following sex.

He also wrote to Mary Loo, saying that he agreed with her

but that he could not take any money from her, for he remembered his grandfather's advice that one should never accept a gift unless one could give as good a one in return. Besides, he was an aristocrat.

When Count Frederick got back to Copenhagen and reported all this, Engelsen threw his plate of pea soup on the floor in a rage.

'Here you go and marry a dollar princess, who even offers you a small fortune as compensation for getting rid of her, and you come back without a penny to your name. Has all my teaching been in vain?'

'My dear Engelsen,' answered the Count, 'my recent experiences with all that is desirable have convinced me that your materialistic theories are wrong. It would therefore have been highly illogical and unphilosophical to saddle myself with the boredom of a small fortune. Besides, it is against my principles to allow myself to be paid off like a gigolo.'

'Your philosophical training is still sadly lacking,' said Engelsen in a tired voice. 'You could have told yourself that wealth is boring only so long as one thinks capitalistically, that is to say egotistically, for then there is no point in money except the satisfaction of one's own desires, which can always be done relatively quickly. But for those of us who think altruistically and socialistically, wealth is quite a different matter, for we continually strive to help others and to set them a shining example. We could have made a little Marxist enclave here in this languishing capitalist community and demonstrated how excellent our theories are in practice.'

'How, for example?' asked the Count.

'We could have bought Egeborg back, made it into a model farm, and given the workers higher wages and better conditions than on any other farm.'

'It is strange how this point of view resembles my grandfather's,' retorted Count Frederick. 'I find it positively attractive.'

'Hm,' said Engelsen, 'they are only alike superficially, and you must not confuse my public utility point of view with that of capitalist success. The fact that Count Hector happened to create a model farm by mere chance only goes to show how meaninglessly the capitalist community functions. But do not let us waste time on these arguments any longer, for after all we have not got the small fortune.'

'Nor any more diamonds,' said Pernille.

'But we still have some rooms to let,' said Count Frederick.

'We could have lived like Sheikh Shir-Mamed and we are finishing up as boarding-house keepers,' said Engelsen, 'and all because the Count does not possess any feeling for the simplest policy of redistribution of income.'

They advertised a room to let in the papers and Engelsen read the two hundred and thirty-three replies right through. When he had made up his mind, he announced with a great air of secrecy that he had accepted an exceedingly interesting lodger.

The day the new lodger arrived Count Frederick opened the door. As she had enclosed a photograph with her reply, he understood immediately why Engelsen had been so sure of his case.

She was the loveliest woman he had ever seen. This was an expression he had used quite often in the past, but this time he really meant it. She had big dark eyes, and as one approached her, they became enormous. He felt as if he were in an express train going through a dark tunnel at high speed. He did not attempt to say anything. He just stood in the open door and gazed at her, which she was evidently quite used to.

'Yes, it is I who have taken the room,' she said. 'I am Princess Maria Medici. I have a big box down in the entrance. Could you bring it up for me, please?'

'Are you a real princess?'

'Yes, quite real. Italian. Didn't you know? You need not look at me as if I were a ghost. There is nothing to be afraid of. I'm afraid I haven't got a kingdom.'

'I am a Count but I haven't got an estate.'

'There you are. But you don't look like a ghost, either.'

Her room lay at the end of a long, dark passage in which the electric bulb was broken, but that did not matter because Princess Maria walked in front of the Count and wore a white dress which shone in the cold darkness. At one time the old flat had been luxurious and beautiful, but now the carpets were worn and the panelling yellow with age, and the big rooms had been divided into many small ones by plywood partitions. But it would not have surprised the Count in the least if Princess Maria had said that she had lived there as a child when this part of the flat was inhabited only by servants. That is to say, if she had been old enough.

A little later she came to him and asked if he would help her move her bed out from the wall.

'I can't bear sleeping in a corner,' she said, 'I hate being cramped. And then do tell me something about the others who live here, and something about yourself.'

Count Frederick tried to tell everything there was to tell, and certainly there was a great deal, but suddenly he dried up. His sentences became telegraphic. Princess Maria sat on the bed and looked at him, and the express train left him breathless. His inside felt hollow and he was ravenously hungry. He rushed out to the kitchen and fetched one of Engelsen's home-baked loaves, cut it in half lengthways and ate it. She would not have any, laughed at him, and said she never ate. She sat very still and listened to all he had to say, but it did not look as if she were really interested, although she insisted that she was. Perhaps she noted down the facts and sorted them out where they belonged. He had a feeling that they did not amount to much and that they were merely being put away in her cold memory, together with a thousand other facts which did not amount to much either. When one looked like that, he thought, there must have been a great deal put away. He felt as if he had just missed a train.

When he told her that he loved her, she smiled in exactly

the same way as she had smiled about the loaf. 'You don't, you know,' she said. 'They all think they do, but later on they discover that they can quite easily leave off.'

'I am quite certain that I can never leave off.'

'Don't say that; so many misfortunes come from that.'

When Engelsen saw her he disappeared for two days, and when he came back he had a very bad hangover. Pellesen declared that one should never go off with anything that one could not bear to part with afterwards.

Engelsen said that he was against princesses in principle but that his principles in this particular case had been seriously shaken. 'One should not go against one's principles,' he declared, 'but neither should one be a slave to them.' When it appeared that she could also make Osso Buco à la Milanaise, he said that there could be no doubt that she was a real princess.

Princess Maria wanted to be a dancer, and naturally she could do whatever she wanted. She earned the money for her training by modelling in an art school, and also for a photographer. Sometimes she danced in a revue chorus, but none of the inhabitants of the flat knew very much about her. At times she was away for several days, and she told no one where she had been.

But the dark old flat became a magical, beautiful place where the strangest things could happen. Count Frederick had a feeling that in some secret room behind a sliding door, which might suddenly open if the right button were pressed, lay hidden the answer to all questions, great and small. He felt that not everything had been in vain — perhaps nothing had been. When they had money they bought wine and they all sat on the floor in Maria's room and got a little drunk, or very drunk, and talked and talked and chased a dream which might suddenly come true.

But this did not happen often, for there were almost always men who telephoned and asked for her, and even when she asked them to say that she was not at home, Count Frederick was often silent and morose from jealousy.

When anyone came to visit her, he was undignified and stupid enough to sit up all night to hear when the visitor went.

'You ought to have pale cheeks, swollen lips, and hatred or mockery in your eyes,' he said.

'No, it all means nothing to me,' she answered. 'I don't think anyone will ever be able to make me any different.'

'Do you want to be?'

'Naturally. One should always be in love.'

'Perhaps I could be of use?'

'No, I'm afraid not,' she said. 'It is you who use me — as a dream.'

'I have written a poem about you,' he said.

'There you are.'

But in spite of the princess's refusal, Count Frederick continued resolutely to believe that he could be of use, and one day when they had money to spend he telephoned the art school and said that Maria had influenza. Then he, Maria, Engelsen, and Pernille, got hold of a car and drove along the coast to Rageleje, where they took a house. It was May, and the house lay right down on the beach. Winter had washed the sand white, the posts in the drying ground had been freshly tarred, and everything smelt clean and new.

Count Frederick and Maria walked along the shore with their bare white feet, and their skin soon became transparent from the water. They piled up heaps of stones and aimed at the topmost one, but Count Frederick always missed. The low crooked pine trees on the high cliffs had light brown finger-stalls on all their shoots, and when these were pulled off, there were soft new green needles underneath. The water was cold, and Engelsen said that he would go up to the house and warm himself with a couple of schnapps before he went in. Pernille went with him. They did not come back.

'Let's go in now,' said Maria. 'There is no one on the beach, so we can bathe without our swimsuits. It is best of all without swimsuits.'

Count Frederick could have eaten two whole home-baked

loaves in one mouthful. She was white and shining like the bark of a birch tree, and her breasts looked as if they weighed no more than blown-out paper bags. She came up to him and kissed him.

'Is it *so* bad?' she asked him.

'It has never been so bad, and it can never be any worse.'

'You are very obstinate,' she said. 'So I can never get away from it?'

'No,' he said, and knew it was the most important thing he had ever said in his life.

'Then there is nothing to be done,' she answered, 'and as long as I can remain a dream all will go well.'

She turned a little to tease him, and the sharp morning sun ran wild hands over her flat belly.

'But we will bathe first,' she said. 'One should always bathe before one celebrates.'

CHAPTER EIGHTEEN

Count Frederick wins the big prize in a television quiz, and the Danish people increase their knowledge of modern culture.

THINGS could not have been better. Count Frederick was perpetually in the seventh heaven, and his soul performed astral gymnastics with the greatest of ease. His happiness infected the others, even though they were naturally a little envious. But they forgot their jealousy when they saw that the Count and the Princess were serious. Engelsen and Pellesen began to accept it as a fact, and their faces became quite kindly because a fixed point had appeared in an otherwise fluid world.

'Unfortunately our economic situation does not match this homeric love which we are all witnessing,' said Engelsen. 'When these two doves suddenly appear with black rings round their eyes because they have had so much to talk about that they have had no time to sleep, I should be able to say to them: "Which vintage do you wish us to have to celebrate your rare appearances? A Chambertin 1904?" And to this the Count ought to answer as follows: "Oh, must we have Chambertin 1904 again? Let us rather have champagne." After which I ought to be in a position to answer in a light, carefree tone: "As you wish. Veuve Clicquot, or Pommery and Greno Sec?" But can we carry on this pleasant conversation? No fear! I am afraid we are very far from the basic rule of Marxism: that one should give according to one's ability and enjoy according to one's need. We must do something about it.'

Pedersen suggested that they should content themselves with a case of Kamanganda Festival Beer, but Engelsen aimed at higher things, and since he was a very gifted man it was not long before he found a solution.

'The quiz!' he burst out one day in a moment of inspiration. 'Of course! We'll send in an application and Count Frederick shall choose modern methods of torture as his special subject. He simply cannot avoid winning, with all his experience. We shall win a fortune, we can buy back Egeborg, and the Count and Princess Maria can get married.'

'And you can at long last marry your beloved Pernille,' said Pernille.

'Yes, of course,' answered Engelsen.

No sooner said than done, and after a test the Count was summoned to the television studios to answer the $64,000 question. The press paid a great deal of attention to the event, partly because the Count was so well-known, and partly because the subject he had chosen was nothing if not educational, thus giving the lie to those conceited intellectuals who maintained that the quiz was culturally beneath contempt. Now, however — the newspapers claimed — we were living in an age when so many political systems used the forms of interrogation known to the Count that it was highly desirable that the Danish people should have a chance of learning more about them. As a result, on the night the programme was presented there was nobody in the streets or in the restaurants and cinemas, and those who had television were inundated by friends and acquaintances, to say nothing of other people whom they scarcely knew but who wished to widen their knowledge.

There had to be two experts as judges, so the television company had first approached the Russian Embassy, who were greatly honoured and promised to send a particularly well-informed official from the Ministry of State Security. Odd though it may seem, he turned out to be none other than Comrade Batjusjov. It was very thrilling for the viewers to see on the screen the happy meeting between the Count and Batjusjov. They exchanged a number of personal remarks which were perfectly audible, and this made the whole programme seem exceptionally spontaneous. Batjusjov said that he had forgiven Pernille for running away from him in

Aden, especially as the Sheikh Shir-Mamed III later gave him rich compensation from his own harem.

The programme's compère, Mr Sven Overstrain, who was very quick in the uptake, interrupted. 'So you have been in Arabia, Comrade Batjusjov?'

'What makes you think that?' asked Batjusjov.

'I *thought* it must be a joke when you said it,' Mr Overstrain said, laughing. 'So far as I know, Arabia is not yet part of the Soviet Union. This is going to be a very lively programme with so much wit here in the studio.'

'What happened to Shir-Mamed II?' asked Count Frederick.

'Oh, he became a head shorter owing to a few misunderstandings about an irrigation plant,' said Batjusjov.

'Got into hot water, did he?' said Mr Sven Overstrain. 'That was a very witty remark. But tell me, who actually was Shir-Mamed II and III?'

'He was a camel,' answered Batjusjov.

'Well, what d'you know! I had no idea that camels had harems,' said Mr Overstrain.

'They don't,' answered Batjusjov.

'But I thought you said — '

'Leave him alone,' said Count Frederick. 'He can't help it.'

Batjusjov shrugged his shoulders and went over to the judges' seat.

'Do you mean me?' asked Mr Overstrain.

'No,' answered Count Frederick. 'The camel.'

Mr Overstrain roared with laughter. 'Perhaps it is ashamed of having a harem?' he suggested.

'Oh my God,' sighed the Count.

'Now then, you're not nervous, are you?' comforted Mr Overstrain. 'It will be all right. I shall help you all I can.'

'Thank you, I hope you will not have to work too hard.'

Mr Overstrain roared with laughter again.

The second judge was a criminologist, Dr Bastiansen, who murmured something about the whole thing being very significant.

'Now, shall we take the first question first?' said Sven Overstrain. 'One should always begin at the beginning, and well begun is half done, isn't it? When the end is good — when the beginning is good — hm — hm ... The first question runs as follows: what is a knout, where is it used, and for what purpose? You need not answer immediately. You have one minute in which to think out your reply.'

'The knout is a Russian whip that my friends and I have unfortunately had ample opportunity to know intimately during a three years' sojourn in the concentration camp of Kamanganda in Siberia,' said the Count.

'Kamanganda is not a concentration camp but a hospital for nervous disorders,' said Batjusjov. 'Otherwise the question is correctly answered.'

'I protest,' said Dr Bastiansen. 'Scientifically, the question consists of three parts, and only the first has been answered.'

'That all sounds terribly scientific,' said Sven Overstrain. 'Couldn't you express yourself a little less technically, Doctor?'

'Psychologically, the most interesting part of the question deals with the purpose of the knout,' said Dr Bastiansen.

'But we are not talking about psychology.'

'If *you* say so, it must be right,' said Batjusjov.

'It is so much talked about nowadays that one can never be quite sure,' answered Mr Overstrain. 'And of course, two birds in the bush are worth one in ... one bird in the hand ... But it says in the television papers that this programme deals with modern methods of torture and I really cannot see what they have to do with psychology.'

Dr Bastiansen then gave a lecture on the psychological significance of sadism. He read it from a manuscript he had brought with him, and finished by saying that he would like a more detailed description of the whip in question than that the Count had given.

'A whip cannot be anything but a whip,' said Sven Overstrain, winking conspiratorially at Count Frederick.

'Indeed it can,' said Dr Bastiansen.

'When is a whip not a whip?' Mr Overstrain cried joyfully.

'Perhaps the Count would kindly answer my question,' said the doctor.

'The knout consists of a short wooden handle to which are fastened a number of leather thongs, each with a metal ball on its end,' answered Count Frederick.

'Correct,' said Sven Overstrain, waving the paper on which the questions and answers were set out. 'That is what it says here, so it must be right.'

'Is there anything special about those leather thongs?' asked the doctor.

'Now I really think we should be satisfied,' said Sven Overstrain. 'We cannot eat our cake and have — er — eat ... isn't that so?'

'By what right do you suddenly speak of yourself in the plural?' Dr Bastiansen asked, and turned to the Count. 'Can you answer my question?'

'The thongs consist of strips of leather, plaited together when wet, because the edges become ragged and as sharp as knives when they are dry,' answered Count Frederick. 'The purpose is to subject the delinquent to a corporal punishment which is administered mainly on the back and buttocks, but in more savage cases on other parts also.'

'Knouts have marked educational properties,' said Batjusjov, and nodded in a friendly way.

'Phnnnnn!' said Dr Bastiansen.

'Now we've suddenly gone all plural ourselves, haven't we?' asked Sven Overstrain.

'*You* have,' said the doctor.

'Why me?' Mr Overstrain asked, and looked round. 'I see no one except us. It is strange how someone we do not know seems to be coming and going all the time. But enough of that. One cannot make bricks without ... Empty vessels make the most ... Etcetera. We may now say that this question has been fully answered. Shall we go on to the next one, Count?'

'Certainly, if the doctor will allow it.'

'Phnnn!' sniffed the doctor.

The Count answered the following question to everybody's satisfaction. Nevertheless Dr Bastiansen managed to take the opportunity of pointing out once or twice that the Count was not always sufficiently scholarly in his explanations. This gave him an opportunity to read the audience two more lectures.

The excitement in hundreds of thousands of homes rose to heights usually reached only during a cup final as the last question was successfully reached.

'Will you kindly go into the Box?' said Sven Overstrain. 'Thank you, thank you. Shut the door, please, and adjust the earphones. Can you hear me?'

No answer.

'Can you hear what I am saying?'

The Count stuck his head out of the box. 'It looks as if you were saying something.'

'Yes, I am. I asked if you could hear what I said.'

'What did you say?'

'I haven't said anything yet.'

'You said you had.'

'I am about to say something. Now I am only asking if you can hear what I say.'

'As long as you haven't said anything, I can't hear it, can I?'

'Ah, but I did say something.'

'In that case, I must ask you once more: what did you say?'

'I am only trying to say that I am now about to say something, and asking whether you can hear what I am saying.'

'So you haven't said anything yet?'

'Yes. I said that I said that I wanted to say something to see if you could hear what I wanted to say.'

'Oh, my goodness,' answered the Count, 'we had better begin again from the beginning.'

He shut the door of the box once more, put on the earphones, and sat down to wait.

'Can you hear what I am saying?' shouted Sven Overstrain.

No answer.

'Hallo, hallo? Can you hear what I am saying?'

The Count popped his head out of the box again. 'Are you still trying to say what you want to say?' he asked.

Sven Overstrain looked as if he was about to burst into tears. 'There must be something wrong with the microphone,' he whimpered.

'You mean you are still talking without saying anything?'

Sven Overstrain stamped his foot and answered angrily: 'I am saying that I said that I said that I wanted to ask you if you could hear what I said when I said that I wished to say something. I cannot understand it.'

'Nor can I,' replied Count Frederick. 'You speak a very strange language.'

'I am not speaking any language at all,' shouted Sven Overstrain. 'I have not said anything yet. Will you get back into that box immediately and keep quiet. This is not a circus.'

'Are you sure of that?'

'Get into that box!' yelled Sven Overstrain. 'Have you ever seen a circus?'

'Is that the question?' the Count asked into the microphone.

'So at last you can hear what I say?'

'Yes, especially if you wouldn't shout so much. All the same, it is a strange question. What has a circus to do with instruments of torture?'

'That is not the question.'

'Then why did you ask me?'

'I didn't.'

'That was what I heard.'

'You heard nothing at all,' hissed Sven Overstrain. 'And you will hear nothing now until I tell you to.'

'Very good,' answered the Count.

'Can you hear what I say?'

No answer.

'Can you hear what I say, blast you?'

No answer.

Sven Overstrain threw down the microphone, and growled: 'It is impossible. I cannot make head nor tail of this. I will not go on with it.'

Then he pulled himself together, ran over to the box, and opened the door so violently that it came off its hinges and fell on top of him. He crawled out from under it, groaning.

'Can't you answer?' he demanded.

'As soon as ever you tell me to,' said the Count.

'I am telling you to now. Do you understand that?'

'That is not difficult.'

'Good. Now I will go over there and ask my question into the microphone, and you must pretend that you cannot hear it except through the earphones, just as if the door were still there.'

Sven Overstrain went over to the other side of the studio, pulling the microphone with him, tripped over the lead, picked himself up, and asked into the mouthpiece: 'Well, here we are. Can you hear what I say?'

No answer.

'CAN YOU HEAR WHAT I SAY?'

No answer.

He turned furiously to the Count. 'Why don't you answer?'

'There is not a sound in the earphones.'

'Yes, but you heard when I asked if you could hear what I said?'

'You have forgotten that you told me that I must pretend I could not hear it except through the earphones.'

'Oh my God,' shrieked Sven Overstrain. He threw the microphone away, and tottered out.

'I'll take over,' said Batjusjov. He opened the envelope and read out the question.

'Describe the electric bulb that burnt in Cardinal Mindzenty's cell before he capitulated, and say how long it burnt for.'

'It burnt for three months two days and eight and a half hours,' said Count Frederick.

'Right,' answered Batjusjov.

A great shout of enthusiasm rose from the audience.

'That is not a complete answer,' said Dr Bastiansen.

'Three months, two days, eight and a half hours and ten seconds,' said the Count.

'Phnnn,' said Bastiansen. 'Can you give a description of the bulb?'

A violent argument broke out between the Count and the doctor about the voltage and wattage of the bulb, whether it was pearl or clear, whether anything was written on the socket, and whether one should include the socket with the bulb, or not. The doctor read a lecture about its *gestalt* psychology, but was interrupted by Batjusjov, who said that he thought it was about time the Count received his cheque for $64,000.

The audience rose and clapped wildly. Batjusjov embraced the Count and handed him a parcel, and said: 'It has been a great pleasure for me to be present at this very instructive quiz, not least in that it has helped to bring a greater knowledge of the working methods of the Soviet Union and the people's democracies to the Danish people. On behalf of myself and my country I therefore have the honour to hand you a little souvenir which will remind you of this happy evening, and which may increase your already great knowledge of modern Leninistic legal practices.'

The Count undid the parcel and drew out a new and pristine knout. Everyone clapped wildly.

'The particular interest of this knout,' continued Batjusjov, 'is that it is not only, as you rightly said, first made wet so that the edges become as sharp as knives when dry, but that the liquid into which it was dipped was in fact a strong salt solution which has crystallized all along the edges. This should have a very special effect. Moreover, we have found, after much research, that if metal squares are sewn on to the leather thongs instead of metal balls, they will considerably enhance the effect. This Russian discovery is very recent, and I think I can promise you that you are the first person in the world to hold this type of whip in your hands. Best of luck.'

Dr Bastiansen also had a gift, but before he handed it over he read a very long speech about the importance of viewing torture in the light of history and criminology. The gift was a collected edition of the works of the Marquis de Sade.

'Look at him! He looks like a king,' Princess Maria whispered to Engelsen. 'He has been given a sceptre and an orb, and now he only needs a kingdom.'

'Egeborg will fill that need,' answered Engelsen.

'You can't get that for $64,000.'

'You forget, Princess, that he has me as his adviser. That means that those two thousand acres of rich arable land are as good as in his possession already.'

The state radio orchestra then began to play, and Princess Maria rushed up and kissed Count Frederick, and it was quite the most moving scene that had ever been seen on Danish television.

CHAPTER NINETEEN

They buy back Egeborg and celebrate a double wedding at which Engelsen makes a very unconventional wedding speech.

ENGELSEN took charge of the cheque and went to the pools expert who still had a room in the flat, and between them they worked out a system which with a stake of $64,000 soon brought in a profit amply big enough to buy back Egeborg with its farm and surrounding fields, and put it into working order again. This required a good deal of capital, because the State had by degrees been forced to sell off all the cattle. The machinery was rusty and out of date, and the stables and barns on the point of collapse, but as the castle was no longer big enough to contain the ever-expanding Ministry for Cultural Exchanges with Friendly Nations, and it was not possible to get permission to increase the resident staff so that the property could again be self-supporting, they were more than willing to sell the lot.

Six months after the eventful quiz, the Count, the Princess, Engelsen and Pernille were able to move into Egeborg and get married. The double wedding took place in the castle chapel, and afterwards there was a big dinner in the banqueting hall for all their friends: Phrederickh Phrederickhsen and his wife, Pedersen, who in the meantime had also acquired a wife, Pellesen with the ship-builder's wife, Mr Ming and his wife, Comrade Batjusjov with three ladies from his harem, A.55 (by kind permission of Mr Larry Loo), Miss Sonja, the pools expert, and Professor Friede.

The writer Ole Windbagsen had declined his invitation.

Everybody was happy and gay. Pernille looked like Pernille and Princess Maria looked like a princess. Engelsen tapped on his glass, and cleared his throat.

'Dear Count and Countess,' he said, 'my beloved bride, friends male and female, today we celebrate what is in reality a highly anachronistic feast. For marriage is not only contrary to nature and a social impossibility: it is also entirely superfluous.'

'Aw, haw, haw,' belched A.55, who had had great success during the last six months in building up a male organ for himself. He was sitting next to Miss Sonja.

'So long as he sticks to words, he can say what he likes,' Pernille murmured to the Count, 'for his hands and other parts of him betray a very different opinion.'

'It is wonderful to do something that is entirely superfluous,' said Countess Maria Peder Wessel Ulrik-Ulrikkenfeldt, winking encouragingly at Engelsen. 'If at the same time it is contrary to nature and a social impossibility, it makes it all the better.'

'That marriage is a social impossibility,' continued Engelsen, 'is clearly demonstrated by the fact that in Copenhagen alone there are about 9,000 marriages a year and about 3,000 divorces, that is to say one third of the total. If we look at the development from 1930 to 1950, note the figures for the increase in population, and then put the number of marriages and the number of divorces in 1930 at 100, we shall get an increase in the population in the course of 20 years from 100 to 121, and in marriages from 100 to 131, whereas the number of divorces rose from 100 to 299. When we add to this the fact that in marriages where both partners are under 25 every other one ends in divorce, then we cannot doubt that, from the social point of view, it is irresponsible to marry. In fact these divorce figures are too low, if we take into account those marriages that are emotionally broken but survive because of lack of money or because of the children or one's reputation. If it were possible to obtain statistical information about this state of affairs — which could be done pretty quickly if the men were given a guarantee that their information would be treated in strict confidence and not divulged to their wives — my guess is that we should find that at least half the existing marriages are hated by the partners, who are all too often the victims of this outworn convention.'

Pedersen, happening to catch his wife's eye, drank the Kamanganda Festival Beer which stood beside his champagne in one gulp, and dispatched a waiter to the kitchen for half-a-dozen more bottles.

'Philosophy is all very well,' said Pernille, polishing her wedding-ring, 'so long as it is treated as an end in itself.'

'Engelsen would make a brilliant psychiatrist or chairman of a commission,' said Phrederickh Phrederickhsen.

'Or a commissar in the Soviet Union,' added Batjusjov.

'Engelsen is best as Engelsen,' said the Count.

'Now none of this would really matter,' Engelsen went on, 'if all marriages were securely anchored in human nature. This, however, is far from being the case. The idiotic part of it all is that marriage can never be anything but a compromise whereby the two partners each sacrifice the best in themselves, that is to say all the refreshing little foibles that make up the independent individual. And there is scarcely anyone of those present who will deny that we all — men especially — are polygamous, and therefore quite unsuited to marriage. It is perhaps the only thing on which we can all agree in this world, apart from nationality, race and political opinions. Below the belt we are, as we all know, brothers.'

'Hear, hear,' said A.55.

'It might still be all right if we regarded marriage as they did in olden days when jealousy was practically unknown,' went on Engelsen. 'Odysseus hardly gave a thought to the numerous divorces of which he was the cause. And wasn't Penelope to some extent responsible for the fact that the house was filled with suitors? And think for a moment of the medieval troubadours who sang always of the love between the knight and his (married) mistress. The romantic idea of love can best be characterized by Friedrich Schlegel's remark that "Love is a child of Bohemianism; it has never recognized its responsibilities." But today, with bourgeois respectability rampant, faithfulness in marriage has been made into something sacred, thereby blocking the only acceptable outlet for matrimonial steam pressure. Today, therefore, matrimony is more pronouncedly unnatural than ever before.'

'God knows who he thinks he is talking about,' said Pernille to the Countess. 'To my knowledge faithfulness has never troubled him, and never will. This is a very abstract and theoretical wedding speech.'

'I think I'd call it a sermon,' said Countess Maria.

'In praise of what?' asked Pernille.

'In praise of Engelsen,' said the Count.

'Your health,' said Pedersen, and refrained from catching his wife's eye.

'People are more amusing than one would expect on the whole,' said A.55, and smiled broadly at Engelsen, while edging closer to Miss Sonja.

'Engelsen is fat and solid and cheerful and the surest proof in this world that everything will be as it has always been,' said Pellesen, and looked tenderly at his ship-builder's wife.

'Instead of embarking on a double marriage here at Ege-borg,' said Engelsen, 'we should have declared publicly that we considered such a ceremony quite superfluous, since logically there are only two possibilities: either two people love each other, or they do not. If they love each other, why should they marry? It will not make them love each other more. If they do not, it is even more absurd to marry — not least because, as we all know, it is better to be well hanged than badly married.'

'Hear, hear,' said Batjusjov. 'The Soviet Ministry of State Security would fully agree with that statement.'

'Besides which, our brides now run the risk of losing their husbands, and as loss of teeth and husbands are said to be the two things that spoil a woman's beauty,' continued Engelsen, 'it is very inconsiderate of us to expose them to this danger. I know that the two brides in question are so endowed by nature that they can afford to lose several husbands before it will be particularly noticeable, but none the less the Count and I have behaved with inexcusable selfishness in this matter.'

'Cheer up, Engelsen,' said Pernille, 'so long as I am running this risk it will be all right. You have never found it very difficult to bear your neighbour's burdens.'

'As the Count and I have assumed this heavy responsibility,' continued Engelsen, paying no attention to the inter-ruption, 'we may perhaps hope that our wives will know how to appreciate it and treat us with that respect merited by men of such inflexible determination. In the hope that I have not miscalculated in this matter — because for some in-explicable reason women do *not* always do exactly the oppo-site of what one expects — I ask you all to give three hearty cheers for the Count and me.'

'Engelsen, I love you,' said Pernille.

The speech provoked a lively debate, to which all con-tributed except Professor Friede. Many cheers were given, many bottles of champagne were drunk, the bridal waltz was danced, and a large number of cases of Kamanganda Festival Beer were carried up from the cellar and Pedersen carried down in their place. Throughout it all the Countess continued to look like a real princess and Pernille's melons swelled out like four fine upstanding postulates, demon-strating that although one may have travelled widely and experienced much, and despite the fact that this world is still far from being the best of all possible worlds, yet it is not possible for man to destroy what Our Lord in his bounty originally created.

When the tower clock struck twelve the Count lifted up his bride, carried her into the Ulrik-Ulrikkenfeldt's bed-room, and laid her in the four-poster bed where all the Ulrik-Ulrikkenfeldts for six hundred years had been born, made love, slept and drawn their last breath.

'It was a good thing you were so pig-headed, after all,' she said.

'I love you,' said Count Frederick.

'Oh,' she sighed, as satisfied as a cat who has been allowed to lick cream, 'tonight there is scarcely time to bathe first.'

CHAPTER TWENTY

In which ends the story of Count Frederick and his friends, the account of the life he led in early youth, and his conclusions resulting therefrom.

EGEBORG was soon its old self again, and became a model estate as in Count Hector's day, and Mr Engelsen, M.A., will no doubt be appointed tutor to the little counts and countesses when they make their appearance, which they obviously will in quick succession. The Count showed all his grandfather's zeal in the computation of interest, and not the smallest piece of land was allowed to lie fallow. The stables were again stocked with prize cattle, and Engelsen again lay alone, or almost alone, and sunbathed on Egeborg beach. Moreover, he very quickly put on even more weight.

'So everything has turned out for the best,' he said, 'and we can wish for no better proof that we are well on the way to the best of all possible worlds.'

'It can scarcely be said to be due to the Marxist theories you used to praise,' answered the Count.

'My dear boy, what is this?' cried Engelsen, horrified. '*Used* to praise! After all we have been through! If Mr Phphrederickh Phrederickhsen had not come to Egeborg and nationalized the land, we should not have gone bankrupt and you would never have become a civil servant in the Ministry for Cultural Exchanges with Friendly Nations and so travelled to the Soviet Union, Spain, Morocco, Libya, Egypt, Syria and Saudi Arabia, nor would you ever have held your position as delivery van driver, or met Mary Loo and lost a million dollars, so that we were forced to let the room to the Countess; and if we had not done that, you would never have got married nor taken part in the quiz so that you could buy back Egeborg. If there had been no welfare state, none of this would have happened.'

'Possibly not,' said the Count, 'but let us rather go down to the cowsheds and inspect the new bull.'